KATE

Also by Valerie Sherrard:

Out of the Ashes (2002)
In Too Deep (2003)

KATE

Valerie Sherrard

A BOARDWALK BOOK
A MEMBER OF THE DUNDURN GROUP
TORONTO · OXFORD

Editor: Barry Jowett
Copy-Editor: Andrea Pruss
Design: Jennifer Scott
Printer: Webcom

National Library of Canada Cataloguing in Publication Data

National Library of Canada Cataloguing in Publication

Sherrard, Valerie
  Kate / Valerie Sherrard.

ISBN 1-55002-476-0

I. Title.

PS8587.H3867K38 2003   jC813'.6   C2003-904048-8

Canada

THE CANADA COUNCIL | LE CONSEIL DES ARTS
FOR THE ARTS | DU CANADA
SINCE 1957 | DEPUIS 1957

ONTARIO ARTS COUNCIL
CONSEIL DES ARTS DE L'ONTARIO

We acknowledge the support of the **Canada Council for the Arts** and the **Ontario Arts Council** for our publishing program. We also acknowledge the financial support of the **Government of Canada** through the **Book Publishing Industry Development Program** and **The Association for the Export of Canadian Books**, and the **Government of Ontario** through the **Ontario Book Publishers Tax Credit** program, and the **Ontario Media Development Corporation's Ontario Book Initiative**.

Care has been taken to trace the ownership of copyright material used in this book. The author and the publisher welcome any information enabling them to rectify any references or credit in subsequent editions.

J. Kirk Howard, President

Printed and bound in Canada.⊛
Printed on recycled paper.

www.dundurn.com

Dundurn Press
8 Market Street
Suite 200
Toronto, Ontario, Canada
M5E 1M6

Dundurn Press
73 Lime Walk
Headington, Oxford,
England
OX3 7AD

Dundurn Press
2250 Military Road
Tonawanda NY
U.S.A. 14150

KATE

Flowers

*Shine sunshine on this field
Gentle breezes, kiss the air
For beneath its smooth, green coat
Lies a lily, pure and fair*

*Sing sweetly little birds
Trill your answer whip-poor-will
Softly sing a lullaby
Slumber on, wee daffodil*

*Dear traveller, stop a spell
Gaze across the solemn rows
Yonder, near a small pink stone
Rests a barely budded rose.*

*Flowers blooming all around
Ah! Your beauty can't compare
To the loveliness we knew
In our sweet pea, resting there.*

~ Mom

CHAPTER ONE

In Farrago the only sirens you ever hear are the police escorting the local sports teams home after a victory game. As long as I can remember, the town has been so quiet you could hear the cats think. (Not my cat though, it's about the dumbest cat in the whole world.)

The people who live here are so law-abiding that you can hardly even find a gum wrapper on the sidewalk unless it blew out of one of the neat yellow trash cans along the street. The police have the easiest jobs of anyone in town, except maybe for Mrs. Collins who works at Bon Appetite, which is the only restaurant in town that has tablecloths. She just shows people where to sit and smiles at them.

Oh, I guess I should have started off by telling you my name, although I really can't see anyone sitting down and reading past an opening sentence like "My name is Marybelle-Anna." Still, you need to call me something don't you? Well, it's *not* Marybelle-Anna, and thank goodness for that one small favour in my life. Not being overrun by blessings, I can at least be grateful that my mother called me something sensible and solid, like Kate, which *is* my name.

There's one other thing I should mention right off, which is that I'm fourteen years old and dying. (I guess that was two things, but the significance of one is sort of tied to the other, don't you think?) I'm not telling you that to get your sympathy or anything, it just doesn't seem the sort of thing you can bring up later on without it looking like you tried to pull a fast one by leaving it out at the start.

I should also tell you that my town's name isn't really Farrago. That's just a word I found in the dictionary one day and took a liking to. It means a confused collection, and that pretty much describes this place.

I don't suppose that too many fourteen-year-old kids read the dictionary, but I can't help that. It's not like I'm a geek or anything — maybe just a bit different from some kids my age. Sometimes when I find a certain word, it feels like an answer to a question I didn't even know I had.

Goodness! I must stop this rambling and get back to the beginning of my story. As I was saying, this place is so peaceful and quiet that the local paper would go broke if it was counting on crime for its news. Instead, we get a lot of pictures and stories of local interest, which, if you ask me, aren't actually all that interesting.

Anyway, when the police sirens started blaring on Saturday afternoon, and there was no sports team coming back into town, people took notice. Before long the streets were buzzing with folks trying to find out what was astir. I heard the news from old Mr. Cafferty, who passed by my veranda on his way home. He was heading back sooner than most of the townsfolk because his rheumatism was acting up and he had to lay down for a spell, but he stopped to give me the news. He had that look that people get when they have something to tell and they know you haven't yet heard it. His chest got kind of big for a minute, and his eyes had a shine of news on them.

"How you doin today young'un?" he asked, although he knows my name full well since we've lived a block from him all of my fourteen years. He didn't wait for me to answer, but went right on with his story, all bursting to let it out. "Quite a thing for a town like this. Yessirree, quite a thing. Have you heard?"

He knew I hadn't heard, since I was sitting there on the veranda and no one else had yet left the crowd he'd just taken himself from, but I allowed as I hadn't, and he nodded importantly, sat down on the rail, and took a handkerchief out of his pocket.

"There's been a robbery!" He wiped his head with the handkerchief as he spoke, mopping drops of sweat that glistened there in the sun. "Leon's garage was held up not half an hour ago by a couple of young hoods passing through. The law has them already, picked them up on the other side of town."

It turned out later that the police had gotten the "hoods," as Mr. Cafferty called them, quite by accident. Mrs. Wickholm's cat had gotten its paw stuck in the big oak tree in their front yard. She had summoned the police, and Officer Peterson was there trying to get the poor thing free when Mrs. Wickholm ran out on the lawn and told him that her sister-in-law had just called with the news that there was a robbery, and he'd better get back to headquarters quick.

The use of the word "headquarters," which is actually a little room with yellow rose wallpaper that the town rents upstairs from Freddy's Barbershop, is not so surprising if you realize that Mrs. Wickholm's husband is the town dentist, a position that allows her to put on some airs and get away with it. After all, none of us are dumb enough to make fun of the woman whose husband is going to have a drill in our mouths at some time or other.

Anyway, Officer Peterson knew his car was low on gas, and worried that a trip to "headquarters" was going to leave him sadly lacking in fuel for a high-speed chase, which I suspect he'd been dreaming about his whole life. He's nice enough, but certainly not the smartest man in town, so when he later described his "quick and clear thinking" I kind of figured it was actually a decision brought on by panic. Instead of racing to the station, he telephoned there for details and found out that the robbery had taken place at Leon's, a gas station just a few blocks away.

Well, when Officer Peterson headed out toward Leon's garage, he was in a rush and took a corner a little too fast. The car swerved and came to rest, blocking the end of the street just as the car carrying the robbers arrived there. (He reported later that he was actually forming a roadblock, knowing full well that this was the most likely way out of town, but Mr. Brown had seen the whole thing and made full use of his observations to gather the attention that he was entitled to for having been walking his dog at that particular moment.)

What happened next becomes confused because a crowd had quickly gathered and there were as many stories as people to witness the event. The nearest I could gather, one of the kids involved in the robbery jumped out of his car and upchucked all over the pavement. His pal was screaming for him to get back in the car, but he just heaved and heaved all over Elm Street. By this time Officer Peterson had managed to get his wits about him, stepped from his patrol car, and announced to the pair that he was taking them into custody. He had his gun drawn, and they must have figured he meant business because they went along quietly.

By the time all the details had floated to my perch, the two were nicely tucked away in the makeshift cell the town had devised primarily for the use of old Berton Mills, who sometimes needs a place to rest after a night at The Pub.

The judge wasn't due to come in until the first of next month, so there were problems right off as to how the town was going to take care of this pair until that time. At a Town Meeting, it was decided that the ladies of the town could take turns making meals to send up to them, at the rate of two dollars for each breakfast and lunch, and four dollars per dinner.

My momma took on dinner three times a week, on Monday, Wednesday, and Saturday. She announced it at the table the next evening.

"Orville," she began nonchalantly, "I've decided that it's my Christian duty to take part in feeding these two lost souls."

"You will do no such thing," my father answered just as casually. I could see that he'd gotten wind of her plan earlier in the day and was ready. "I will not have any member of my family exposed to the criminal ele-ment of society."

My little brother, Mark, took this opportunity to lean over and ask me in a whisper, "Think she'll have to cry to get her way?"

"Hard to say," I hissed back quick, not wanting to miss anything.

"Suppose," Momma said, "it was our own boy, fallen astray, and in need of nourishment and kindness to bring him back to the right path."

"I ain't robbing no gas station," Mark said indignantly.

"You aren't robbing *any* gas station," Momma corrected. She turned back to Daddy. "I hear that one of the boys is an orphan, Orville. Apparently he's been raised by family members, shuttled from home to home with no one really wanting him. I think that calls for some mercy, don't you?"

I watched Daddy's face as soon as I heard the word "orphan" and saw that he knew he was licked. He sighed and threw up his hands. "Do what you feel you must, Lillian." he muttered. And so, it was settled, with no great surprise to anyone at the table. Momma hardly ever argues with Daddy, but when she does, she wins.

When Momma's turn came for the first meal to be sent up, I begged to be allowed to deliver it. At first she was much opposed to it, and I had to get my lower lip trembling before she agreed to let me. I confess that it wasn't as important to me as all that, but in any case, she gave in.

"If your father finds out that you've been there, he'll raise the roof right off the house," she warned, passing me the hamper of food.

"I'll be back long before Daddy gets home," I promised, wondering what on earth Momma had packed in the hamper. It weighed a ton.

I hurried out before Momma could change her mind, and walked along the street with my insides all excited to be going to see real, honest-to-goodness criminals.

I knew that Officer Olson had the afternoon watch, and my chances of actually getting to see the robbers were good because of that. Any other cop in town would have taken the hamper and made me wait in the outer room, but Officer Olson is notoriously lazy and never stands when he can sit.

It was a little hard lugging the hamper up the steep flight of stairs and I had to stop and rest twice. It's hard to get my breath sometimes. Finally, I was at the top, facing a dimly lit hallway that ended at a door, sadly in need of paint and sporting a tarnished bronze sign that reads "Farrago Police Station."

I turned the knob and found myself looking at Officer Olson, tilted back in a chair with his feet on the desk. He had a magazine in his hand, but he tossed it down when he saw me standing there.

"Good afternoon, Officer," I said respectfully. "I've brought dinner up. Shall I just take it in? Momma told me to make sure what she's made is suitable so she'll know whether to send the same again some time." The last was a lie, but it offered him a chance to let me go in without seeming to shirk his duty. He grabbed it happily.

"Go on ahead then, if your Momma instructed you to do that," he said, waving his hand toward the back room. "I'll be right here. If you need me just holler."

"Yes, sir," I said. "Thank you, sir."

We'd had a tour of the police station when I was in grade four, so I knew what to expect. A short hall turned at the end and faced the single cell. It had been roomy enough when I'd seen it for the first time, but appeared much smaller now. I realized at once that was because besides the one cot that was usually there, a second had been added along the other wall. This left a space in the middle of maybe three feet, which now formed a path to the sink and toilet along the back wall.

Over the sink was a tiny window, which didn't let in much light to add to the single light bulb that hung suspended in the middle of the room, with a dirty looking string dangling from it.

The cell had a front of bars, which the town had made from some kind of pipes, but the door was a normal metal type, so you had to stand to the side of the door to see in. This looked rather comical — having a door in the middle of a see-through wall. On the left side there was a break in the bars about halfway up, forming a rectangle of about ten inches wide by three inches deep. It was through here that the meals would have to be passed, and I went to the opening and sat the hamper down to unpack it.

The two young men in the cell looked up without much interest as I knelt at the hamper. Their appearance surprised me. I don't know exactly what I was expecting, but they sure weren't it. Both could have been students at the high school two blocks to the right. They wore blue jeans and T-shirts and had faces that were perfectly average. I glanced up, trying to find some sign of the sinister evil that made them criminals, but their answering looks were lacking in anything but boredom.

"Whatcha got there, kid?" The fellow who spoke didn't look more than seventeen. He was thin, with a pale complexion, light brown hair, and hazel eyes. Across from him, half lying on the other bed, was the second youth, taller but equally thin, with dark skin, eyes, and hair. I knew right off that it was the younger, paler fellow who had puked on the street.

"Dinner for eight, by the feel of this basket," I answered, pulling the lid off and peering inside. At my words the younger boy came over to the bars and looked at me closely.

"You're a *girl*," he said, with unflattering surprise in his voice.

"Well, we all have to be one or the other," I answered shortly, "and I do believe when I was born the doctor informed my mother that she'd been blessed with a female child."

"A girl with a mouth," he added with a backward glance at his partner. He turned back to me. "Why's your hair so short then?"

"Chicken," I announced, pulling out two foil-wrapped shapes that were clearly half a chicken each. "My momma cooks it just right too." I pushed the two shapes through the opening, set them on the rickety table that sat just on the other side, and turned back to the hamper.

"I asked you how come your hair was so short," he repeated.

"And I ignored your question, which should tell any halfways intelligent person that I don't consider that your business," I replied, drawing four thick slices of homemade bread wrapped in waxed paper out and sliding them through the opening.

"Lice," said the dark-haired boy. "Sometimes they cut your hair all off if you get head lice. She was probably crawling with them. Fleas too, likely."

"Fleas," I told him, "reside on animals, not humans, and I have never had head lice in my life. What's more, if you want your dessert, you'd better find some courtesy

19

in that mouth of yours. Otherwise the pigeons are going to enjoy the nice lemon pie I see here in the hamper."

He sneered, but said nothing more. Instead, he turned his back and tried to look fascinated with the wall. The younger boy smiled, but not before a nervous glance at his partner told him it was safe to do so without detection.

"Well, might I ask what your name is?" he said with exaggerated politeness.

"Kate," I answered, placing the last of the food on the table. From the bottom of the hamper I drew out serviettes, paper dinner plates, and plastic cutlery.

"I'm Randy," he said. "Say, Kate, will you be coming up again some time?"

"I might," I answered. It was on my tongue to ask why he wanted to know, but I held it back at the last second.

"If you do," he said, with the first gleam of light I'd seen in his eyes, "could you bring me a book?"

The request so surprised me that I know I stared for a minute, good upbringing and all. He didn't look the sort who read, but here he was asking for a book, and there was hope in his eyes.

"What kind of a book?" I asked. I felt that sense of longing I got when I discovered other book lovers and wanted them to like the same kinds I did. So far no one my age had fit that description.

"Sissy books," the dark-haired youth said nastily. "I swear Randy, you always make a fool of yourself." His voice changed now to mocking, and he added, "Oh, a book! Please bring me a book."

"Well, it's boring in here, Paul," Randy said defensively. "I just want something to help pass the time."

Paul made a rude remark followed by more mimicking, only this time he threw in several obscenities. Randy reddened and looked at me with apology.

The desire for a book won out over his friend's ridicule and he said in a low voice, "Anything you have would be okay. I like some more than others but it doesn't matter, really. I'd sure appreciate it."

I turned this over in my head that night and had a hard time getting to sleep. I don't know why it mattered, but there was something in me that was scared I'd take him a book that he wouldn't like.

Chapter Two

Did you ever see a waterwheel? I did once, when we went on a family vacation. I remember watching the motion, steady and smooth, and thinking that it was a serene kind of movement. As long as there was no commotion of any kind, like if the water began to rush faster, or stopped, or changed direction, it would just keep on, peaceful and steady.

That was two summers ago, and I guess you could say my life was like the waterwheel then. It just moved along with nothing ever happening to cause any commotion. No one paid any particular mind to me. Heck, I didn't really pay much mind to myself! I just went along from day to day. I guess I had the idea that it would always be like that. To tell the truth, I didn't think much about it.

When I was diagnosed, the water changed direction. All of a sudden my life wasn't normal anymore. I was different from the people around me. I started to pay attention to things. A lot of attention. And I sort of got a feel for changes.

I had a feeling that meeting Randy was a shift in my life and that it might be important. And I just plain didn't want that feeling to be wrong. Like I said, little things matter to me.

It might seem silly to you for someone to read that much into a thing as simple as someone asking for a book. I said earlier that I was scared in a funny way that he wouldn't like what I took. That was a selfish fear, mind you. I just wanted to have someone, even if it was just for a little while, who would feel what I feel when I read certain books. I guess I sound like a snob or something, but it's not that I think I'm some great intellect or anything. I just see things differently than most of my friends.

I must have looked through my book collection a hundred times between that Monday and Wednesday, when the next meal would be delivered.

Right up to the time that Momma called me to take the hamper that Wednesday I struggled with it. Twice I decided on *The Catcher in the Rye* only to put it back. And then it struck me. If Randy was the orphan, as I suspected, what would be more perfect to take to him than *Oliver Twist*? I put aside the notion that it might offend him. After all, it's the seeing of ourselves that reaches us in books.

I took it downstairs and sat it on the end table in the hallway, so Momma wouldn't see me take it. I knew she'd have a cat if she knew I was actually talking to the criminals. Momma's progressive attitude, as she likes to call it, hasn't progressed as far as all that. Then it occurred to me that he might like some blank paper too, just in case he liked to write things down when he was reading, or just thinking about things. I do that a lot and it sort of helps me to keep things straight in my head. So I added a blank notebook and a pen.

The hamper wasn't as heavy that day as it had been the first time I delivered it. I was too anxious to get going to bother asking why, but I found out anyway, on the way to the jail, from Mrs. Morrison.

Mrs. Morrison is a neighbour of ours. She lives alone in a big white house three places away. I like her. When the news of my illness spread around town a lot of people told me not to give up hope, to pray for a miracle and stuff like that. Others just ignored it except for the fact that when I was around they were a little too normal or a lot too jovial. But not Mrs. Morrison. She called me up on her step one day and told me that I shouldn't make too much of it.

"Katherine, my dear," she said (she always uses people's full names), "we will all die at some time or other. It may seem unfair to you that your time is coming at such a young age. But the real tragedy would be if you allowed it to make you bitter and therefore wasted the time you have left. Live each day and close your eyes each night with the knowledge that you've spent the hours well. That's all any of us can do. Don't use fate as a cause to be unhappy, for it was never meant to be that way."

"Yes, ma'am," I said, surprised to hear anyone speak so frankly about death. Even Momma and Daddy kind of avoided talking about it right out like that.

"And, Katherine," she continued, "I want you to know that when your time comes, I shall sincerely miss you. Now, come away in and have a glass of lemonade."

And that was it. She never mentioned it again, but treated me the same way she always had, and that was a big deal to me, though I can't fully explain why.

This day she was sitting on her veranda, motionless in the wooden swing chair. I might not have noticed her at all in my haste to get to the jail, but she called out to me as I passed by.

I turned, almost reluctantly, at the sound of my name. For once, being impatient to hurry on, I didn't feel like visiting with her, but I went up the stairs anyway and greeted her.

"Are you off to the police station, dear?" she asked.

"Yes, ma'am. My momma is sending meals to the prisoners three times a week."

"It's no longer prisoners," she corrected mildly. "One of the young men's family has posted bail."

"Oh, well, I'd better run along and get this there before it gets cold," I stammered. I crossed my fingers as I set off, hoping with all my might that it was Paul who was gone, and not Randy.

When I rounded the corner to the cell and saw him sitting there, shoulders slumped and head bowed, I got this funny feeling in my stomach. I figured it was relief, but then you can't always tell what you're feeling, can you?

He saw movement in the hall and glanced up. He looked like he was going to smile, but kept himself from it.

"Hi, Kate," was all he said as I sat the hamper down and kneeled by it. I felt a burn of resentment for a moment that he hadn't seemed glad to see me, considering that I was bringing him a book. But then I figured maybe he was just feeling extra bad now that he was all alone, locked up in that place.

"Hi yourself," I said, forcing a grin. "I see that Mr. Personality has moved out of the Farrago Hilton."

"Paul's not so bad," he said. "I know he has an attitude, but he hasn't had much of a chance in life. His mom and dad are dead you know."

"*Paul's* the orphan?" I asked in surprise.

For a moment he just looked at me. Then he put back his head and laughed. I laughed too, because he was laughing in a way that makes you want to join in, even when you don't know what the joke is. I had a sneaking suspicion that it was on me.

"Oh, that's rich," he said, finally getting control of himself. "So you heard one of us was an orphan and had me pegged for it, did you?"

I didn't know what to say to that. I could feel warmth crawling up my neck and hated knowing I was blushing, but that's not the kind of thing you can do much about, is it? A question that came to my mind right then sort of saved me a little, though. If you just stand there and feel stupid, you're bound to blush even worse, but if you distract yourself it's not as bad.

"If Paul has no parents, who posted bail for him?" I asked.

"His uncle," Randy said. "He owns a gravel business back home. Paul had been staying with them for the past year, but his uncle's wife didn't like him around her own kids, so Paul mostly spent his time at my place. I think his uncle felt guilty that they didn't really like Paul, and that's what made him post the bail. But you should have heard the speech he gave when he picked him up."

"Well, robbing an honest man isn't exactly something you'd want to praise a person for," I said. I regretted it as soon as it was out of my mouth, but that's another thing about me. My daddy says I speak first and think later.

"No, it isn't," was all Randy said to that. I imagined I could see him draw into himself, and tried to think of something to undo it.

"I didn't mean to judge you," was all I could come up with. It sounded lame even to me.

Randy sort of half smiled, but there was no humour in it. "It's not a question of judging," he said quietly. "This is a black and white thing. We did something wrong. It's just a plain fact."

"Will your folks be bailing you out?" I asked.

"No." The way he said it kept me from any more questions on that subject, although I had some in me all right.

"Oh! Your supper's going to be cold," I said, suddenly remembering the hamper at my feet. "I think Momma made pork chops today."

"Tell your momma I appreciate the trouble she's going to," he said. There was something sad in his voice, and I wondered if he was thinking of his own mother.

"I remembered to bring a book," I told him as I pushed the food through to the table. "And some paper in case you wanted to write anything."

"That was kind of you. Thanks," Randy said, coming to the opening. "I'd sure be grateful if you could bring an envelope and stamp the next time. I can pay you for it later."

I passed the paper and pen through and stood holding the book. Now that I knew he wasn't the orphan, I regretted my choice. I felt sure he'd know why I'd chosen it, and wondered what his reaction would be, especially considering his amusement earlier.

His eyes were on the book, and they had a look of eagerness that made a strange pain start up inside me. I passed it to him reluctantly.

"*Oliver Twist*!" he exclaimed with obvious delight. "I love Dickens, Kate. Thank you so much."

"Have you read it already?" I asked.

"Sure. But that doesn't matter. I can read Dickens' books over and over and still enjoy them. I must have read *A Tale of Two Cities* ten times."

I figured I'd already put my foot in my mouth earlier, and since that was the case I might just as well keep it there. "If you'll pardon me saying so," I blurted, "a person who loves Dickens doesn't seem the type to hold up gas stations."

Randy laughed again. "And what type of person *does* hold up gas stations?" he inquired.

"Well, bad guys I guess. How can someone who loves books be a bad guy?"

"I don't know, Kate," he said, now solemn, "if I can explain to you what I can't completely explain to myself. I guess all I can say is that there are two sides to everyone, and in this case the bad side of me won over."

"And what makes the bad side of a person win over the good side?" I asked with real interest.

"Circumstances, I imagine," Randy said. "Hard things in a person's life can make them angry enough to stop caring about what's right, and then they just want to get revenge of some sort for what they're feeling." I was silent and after a moment he added, "I don't suppose a little girl like you would know anything about the hard things in life, so it's probably not something you can understand."

I just shrugged at that. It makes me mad when someone thinks they can figure a person out just by looking at them. Everyone has things that go on inside them, and you just never know what those things might be. So it's a mistake to assume you can know what someone else feels, or has been through, ever.

"I'd better get going," was all I said. He thanked me again, and gave a little wave as I was turning the corner out of his sight.

I got over being mad at Randy about halfway home. After all, if you're fourteen and dying, you're bound to have figured out some things that other people haven't.

CHAPTER THREE

I figured I'd have made five or six trips to the jail before Daddy discovered I was going, but that night at the supper table I found out, and not for the first time either, that it's pretty near impossible to keep anything secret in a small town.

He was reaching for the biscuits, just as casual as you please, when he said to Momma, "Lillian, what's this I hear about Kate delivering the meals to those hoodlums?"

When I thought about it later I realized Momma had been expecting this and had prepared for it. She looked up with the most innocent face in the world and said, "Yes, dear, she is. It saves me going at a time when I'm busy making dinner for my own family. She's been a real help."

Daddy looked like he didn't quite believe his ears. "Tarnation, Lillian," he growled, "I'd have thought you had more sense than to send a child around the likes of that. I don't want her going there again."

"I don't see what the harm is, Orville," Momma said calmly. "All she has to do is drop a hamper off with the officer on duty."

"In the future, you have it ready for when I get home and I'll run it up before I have my own dinner," Daddy said.

I felt my heart sink inside me. There seemed nothing to lose now, so I decided to risk telling the truth. The truth as they'd like to see it, that is.

"Actually, Momma, I've talked to the prisoners," I said.

Before I could get another word out, Mark turned to look at me with big eyes and made my case weaker with a single awestruck, "Wow!"

"Mark!" I said sharply. "There is nothing to admire in criminals, so I hope that wasn't meant the way it sounded."

He's pretty smart, my little brother. He could see right off that he'd said the wrong thing, and he hastened to fix it. "No, Kate, course not," he said with his mouth full of pork chop. "I meant that it was brave of you to talk to them, that's all."

"Mark, be so kind as to refrain from talking when your mouth is full," Momma said automatically.

"Yes, Momma," said Mark, showing more pork.

It wasn't going well, with all the distractions, but I plunged in again, feeling half desperate. "There's only one prisoner left there now. The other one got bailed out. I think he was the one behind it all too, because Randy is really remorseful and ashamed about what he did."

"Randy," snorted Daddy. "Do you hear that, Lillian? Our daughter is on a first-name basis with a criminal."

"Oh, Daddy," I said, trying to make light of it. I knew full well that I was failing miserably, and that the more I said the worse it was getting, but I couldn't stop. "I just take the food in and say a few words and that's all there is to it. I feel like I'm doing a good thing, going there and talking to him a bit."

"And what exactly do you and this, this *person*, talk about?" Daddy's tone of voice didn't put me at ease any, let me tell you. I had the feeling he expected me to say we were planning a heist together as soon as he got out.

"Books, mostly," I said. "He likes Charles Dickens! It's good for me to have someone my own age to talk to about fine literature."

"Good for you? *Good* for you?" Daddy was starting to steam now, and I knew what was coming next before he said it. "I'll tell you what's good for you, young lady. Respectable company. Decent friends. That's what's good for you. I'll not have any child of mine keeping company with criminal elements." He cleared his throat, saw my mouth opening, and added, "There's nothing more to say on the subject."

I looked to Momma for help, but her mouth was closed in a thin line and she turned her eyes down as soon as I gave her a pleading look.

I knew I'd made a big mistake in not telling Momma about talking to Randy before now. I might have been able to win her over, and if she'd taken my part I'd have stood a chance. But I could see she wasn't happy about my keeping it from her, and wasn't prepared to be an ally.

A heavy silence sat on the room for the rest of the meal, and as soon as I'd eaten I asked to be excused. I was all mixed up inside as I washed the supper dishes, and couldn't sort out what I was feeling.

I find the best thing to do when I'm like that is to take a walk along the river, and that's where I headed as soon as my chores were finished.

I really meant to go to the river. I did. But somehow as I got near the water I found my steps turning back. I think maybe I knew the calm of the water would soothe me, and I wasn't quite ready to be soothed. Anyway, the next thing I knew, I was cutting through the back alley behind the police station, and soon found myself looking up at the tiny window of Randy's cell.

The light was on there, and I imagined him reading the book I'd taken. Without thinking of what I was going to say, I picked up a pebble and threw it up against the windowpane. He appeared there after a few seconds and peered around until he saw me waving at him. I signalled him to open the window.

"Hey, Kate," he said in a loud whisper. "What are you doing there?"

"I don't know," I whispered back. "My Daddy said I can't bring your meals up anymore, and I guess I came to tell you that."

"You guess you came to tell me that?" he replied.

"I guess I came to tell you something else too," I said. He waited silently. "I guess I came to tell you that I don't think you're a bad person."

He didn't answer for a minute, and I felt mighty foolish, standing there in the near dark, waiting. I was about to turn and go when he spoke again.

"Kate," he said softly, "I wish I wasn't in here. I wish I'd never done what I did. But I'm glad I got to meet you. It would be neat if we could have been friends."

I felt this strange quiver in me, like you get when you're thinking of doing something daring, and you want to, but you don't. I hardly knew what to make of it.

"Well, I guess I won't see you anymore," I said. "I hope that everything turns out okay for you though, and that you have a good life when this is all over."

"Thank you, Kate," he said. He said it solemnly, like I'd blessed him or something.

On the way home I wished I could have thought of something wise and meaningful to say to him instead of standing there like an idiot and telling him to have a good life. It happens to me that way all the time. I can always think of *remarkable* things to say after the fact, but at the time something is happening, my head goes pretty much blank.

I couldn't get to sleep that night at all. I laid in my bed and tried to think of sleepy things the way I do when it's hard to rest my mind. Usually this works. I think about water rippling and get a picture of it in my head that's as lulling as the real thing. Or I imagine myself lying in a field under the warm sun with just the slightest breeze blowing, just enough to make the tall grass sway in a gentle, hypnotic way. And the next thing I know, I'm waking up.

Not this night though. The more I tried to think of other things, the more Randy kept coming into my head. I could see him, alone there, reading, or maybe just lying flat on his back with his arms folded under his head and staring at the ceiling, thinking his private thoughts. It gave me the oddest feeling, like I wanted to touch his hand or something, just so he wouldn't feel so alone.

Breakfast the next morning was a trying event, let me tell you. I was grumpy from lack of sleep and wanted to be left alone. But Daddy was bound and determined that he was going to make up for what he'd denied me the night before. I've noticed that grown-ups do that a lot. They think that they can substitute something in the place of what you really want, and it will satisfy you. It never does, but they don't seem to notice.

"Kate, my girl," he said jovially. "I was thinking it's been a while since we went fishing together. How's about we pack a lunch this Saturday, why that's tomorrow isn't it, and take the boat out?"

"No, thank you," I said. I said it with forced politeness, and made sure it sounded like forced politeness.

"Why, Kate, you love fishing," Momma said, trying to smooth things over.

Like I don't know how much I love fishing, and needed to be informed of it. Don't you hate it when someone tells you that you love something? It's the same as when someone offers you something to eat that you don't want.

"Would you like a piece of chocolate cake?"

"No, thank you."

"But you love chocolate cake."

What, do they think you don't know that? If you love chocolate cake and refuse a piece, it should tell the person something. Maybe you're full, maybe you have a toothache, maybe you just don't like the way they *make* chocolate cake. Why try to make a person feel guilty by using their own likes against them? It's just plain stupid if you ask me.

Anyway, I'm rambling here. I seem to do that a lot, don't I? But if you're fourteen years old and dying, you get the feeling that you have to cram everything in as fast as possible.

So, Daddy's face wasn't looking any too pleased. I'd cheated him out of his chance to get rid of his own guilt by not taking the offer. He decided to turn the blame on me.

"You're going to sulk, are you, Kate?"

I said nothing, and tried to look fascinated with my corn flakes, which were rapidly getting soggy.

"Your father asked you a question," Momma pointed out. Momma can be a master of bringing your attention to the obvious.

"It didn't seem the sort of question that wanted an answer," I said. "But if you insist on having one, here it is. I'm not sulking. I'm disappointed because I don't feel it's fair that I can't talk to someone if I want to. And I want to be left alone."

I forgot for a moment what a dangerous thing it can be to tell your mom and dad that you want to be left alone. Parents never take that at face value from a child. They redouble their efforts to cheer you up, and can darn near drive you crazy in the process.

"Well, if you don't want to go fishing with your father," Momma began her campaign right away, "maybe you'd like to go shopping with me instead. We can pick out material for some new kitchen curtains, and have lunch at Bon Appetite."

"I was thinking maybe I'd go over to Josie's place for the day," I said. It was a lie though, since the thought hadn't even occurred to me until that moment.

Momma and Daddy exchanged "well, we tried, we did our best" looks and dropped it. I finished my corn flakes and went out on the veranda. Sammy, our cat, was sunning himself out there and, as if he was in on the conspiracy to cheer me up, came over and rubbed against my legs.

I was scratching Sammy's face, along the side the way he likes, when Mark came out. He came to my side and laid his head against my shoulder. I leaned my face down in his hair. His hair smelled fresh and clean from shampoo and sunshine.

"Hey, Kate," he said, "do you wanna walk down by the river and look for bottles with messages in them or something?"

We do this sometimes, during summer vacation. We've never found any bottles with messages, but we've come across some neat shells, rocks, and pieces of driftwood. We used to talk about what kind of message we might find in a bottle, and even wrote a few in our own and sent them off with our name and address inside, but we never got any answers.

"Okay," I said. An idea came to me, and I told him

to wait while I ran upstairs for a moment.

We started off along the street, but when we got to the field we cross to get to the river, I told him we were taking a detour first.

"We going to the library?" he asked, noticing the book in my hands.

"Nope," I said, "we're going on a secret mission."

"To the prisoner!" he said, eyes shining.

"Hush your mouth," I said sternly. "Is that any way for a secret agent to act, hollering out top secret information on the street?"

"Sorry," he whispered. I hugged him quick, which is the only way a little brother generally lets you hug him.

When we got to the jail I wanted to leave him downstairs, but it wouldn't have been fair to him. I knew if Momma and Daddy found out I'd taken him there it wouldn't be too good for me, but sometimes you have to take a chance.

His eyes were big with excitement as we climbed the stairs to the police station.

"I'll be talking in a secret code," I whispered, "so just let on that you don't know anything's up."

He nodded and we went inside.

Officer Johnson was on duty that morning. He looked up as we came in and held up a finger to say just a minute.

"Yes, dear," he said, talking into the phone, "I've

got it written down right here. I won't forget." He paused, glancing at us, and then read from a paper in front of him, making his voice as low as possible, "Milk, butter, a can of spaghetti sauce, and toilet paper." Another pause, and then, "I've got business to take care of now. I'll talk to you later." Another pause. "Yes, I love you too."

Officer Johnson had only been married for a couple of months.

"Good morning, Officer," I said cheerily. "I've brought up a book for your prisoner. Momma said to leave it with you. She said it would be good for him to take this opportunity to improve his mind, so that he can become a productive member of society some day."

"Your mother is a good Christian woman," Officer Johnson said, taking the book from me. "I'll see that he gets it right away."

"Thank you sir," I said. Mark and I ran down the stairs, giggling at our success.

Once out on the pavement he turned to me. "You got any money?"

"I can't hear you," I said. It's a sort of habit I got into with him, to help him learn to talk right.

He squinted, thinking for a moment. "Do you *have* any money?" he tried again.

I reached into my pocket and pulled out a worn two-dollar bill and some change. "Three bucks," I said after I'd counted it.

"All I've got is forty-seven cents," he said with a sigh. He dumped his change into my palm. "Can we get something at the soda shop before we go to the river?"

"Hey, secret agents deserve a treat after doing a special assignment," I said.

"Race you there?" he challenged.

"Not today, Mark." I knew I didn't have to explain it to him. He just nodded, fell into step with me, and off we went.

Chapter Four

I went down to Josie's place the next morning, as early as I could. I guess I should tell you a little bit about Josie before I go any further.

Most of the people in Farrago have lived there all their lives. Not Josie's family. They moved here when I was in the third grade. Her father had bought old Mr. Parker's hardware store.

This didn't sit well with Mr. Parker's son-in-law, Jeff Richards. He'd married Mr. Parker's daughter, Maryanne, who was no beauty by anyone's standards, and had worked for the old man for almost six years before Josie's father came along and bought the business.

The next thing, Jeff Richards had up and left. Just like that. Maryanne Richards, who had gotten rounder each year, quickly became a recluse, and before long, she completely stopped leaving the bungalow she had shared with her husband. She had groceries delivered and directed all of her bills to her father. This was the only communication he ever had from his only child. Mr. Parker stopped by every Sunday after church and rang her doorbell, but Maryanne never answered the door. Not for him — not for anyone.

I guess I've wandered off subject again though. I was telling you about Josie, and when her family came to Farrago. The school year had already started when her father brought the rest of the family and moved them into the old United Church manse. The church had built a new, more modern house to use as a parsonage, and the old manse had been up for sale for nearly three years when Josie's father bought it. It was a big, rambling house with six bedrooms, and the young couples in Farrago were inclined to want smaller homes.

It would be hard to forget the first day that Josie came to school. The teacher, Mr. MacDougall, introduced her to the class. She stood there at the front of the room with her face as red as her hair, looking as though she'd like to crawl under the desk.

"Say hello to Josie Spencer," Mr. MacDougall instructed.

"Hello Josie," we chorused, with the lack of unity only a group of eight year olds can achieve.

"Say hello to the class, Josie," Mr. MacDougall encouraged.

Well, Josie didn't say hello. What she did instead was pee her pants and begin to sob.

Mr. MacDougall is a nice man, and he did his best under the circumstances, ushering Josie out of the room and sending for her mother. He returned to the class, which stopped laughing when they saw his disapproval, and gave us a speech on kindness. He told us to pretend it had never happened when Josie came back to school.

He might just as well have saved his breath.

For months Josie was reminded daily at recess of her disgraceful entry into Farrago. She spent most of her time hiding from her tormentors, and at noon hour she sat alone with her lunchbox and a book, which she mostly used to hide behind.

The book she chose was an atlas, borrowed from the library, no doubt for its size. The boys would pass by her table and ask her if she was looking for new places to go pee her pants. She never looked up or let on that she heard them, but her face would flush.

At that time I was part of a group of girls who had little sympathy for Josie's predicament. They didn't chase her and call her names like the boys did, but when she walked past they would make a *shhhhhsplash* sound and giggle.

"Maybe we should be nice to her," I suggested one day when Josie's suffering had finally started to get to me. "After all, she's new in town and everything."

"Oh, brother!" Peggy said with disgust. "Do you really want to be around someone who pees her pants like a baby?"

"Yeah," said Connie. "Anyway, the boys would start teasing us too."

"But how do you think she feels?" I asked.

"Wet," Connie said, to a burst of laughter.

I said nothing else for more than a week, fearing the ridicule of my friends, and not wanting to risk losing them. But every day I would see Josie's face, full of shame and set in a determined "I don't care" look, and finally I just couldn't take it anymore.

The next day when I got to the lunchroom I walked past the table where my friends sat and seated myself across from Josie at her table. I could hear a murmur from the other girls, and it was a scary sound, let me tell you. I knew that I'd taken a step I couldn't undo, but something in me felt good and proud and free for it.

Josie ignored me at first. I think she figured I was there as some sort of dare, or to humiliate her up close or something. But after a while she put her book down and looked right in my face. I smiled at her, and it was the weirdest thing, but I found myself feeling really shy. It wasn't the feeling I'd expected to have, being her rescuer and all.

After that, I ate with Josie every day, and we finally got some conversations going and found out that we really liked each other.

It took a long time before Josie got to be accepted by the other kids. In the meantime I was pretty much left out of things too, but it wasn't like a sacrifice at all. Josie was a better friend than anyone I'd known before, and as long as we had each other to play with and talk to, we didn't feel any lack for other company.

When Josie got to be thirteen, something wonderful happened. She blossomed. And I do mean blossomed. Her skin got this creamy glow, her hair deepened a shade into a beautiful dark red, and she got a figure. Suddenly, everyone wanted to be around her. The boys made fools of themselves over her, and the girls envied and adored her all at once. I was downright proud of her.

The big thing missing in our friendship is that she isn't interested in books and writing like I am. She finds it hard to understand how I get all emotional reading certain things, and she never even cried when we read "The Highwayman" together.

They say that opposites attract, but we aren't opposites. We have lots in common, and some differences. Mostly, we just like each other a lot and don't worry about the things that aren't there, which is what makes any friendship work.

When I got to Josie's place that Saturday morning, I found the house silent. The door was open, so rather than knock and wake everyone, I just went in and tiptoed up to her room. She was sleeping, kind of curled up like a baby.

"Josie," I whispered. She stirred and opened her eyes, squinting at me.

"Hi," she said sleepily. "What time is it?"

"Ten to eight."

She groaned and shut her eyes. I just sat and waited, and after a minute she opened them again and stretched.

"Gee, Kate, what are you doing here so early?" she asked.

"I just had to get out of the house today," I told her. "My mom and dad are trying to make up for not letting me go to see Randy anymore, and they're getting on my nerves."

She sat up, rubbing her eyes. "Who?"

"The guy in jail," I said, half annoyed that something that mattered to me had gone so quickly out of her head.

"Oh, yeah." She yawned and slid out of bed. "Well, I don't think it's fair, considering." She blushed as soon as she'd said that. Josie doesn't quite know how to handle my upcoming demise, you know, and any time she says anything that makes some sort of reference to it she gets flustered.

"They might yet give in, considering," I laughed. It was the only hope I had on the subject, but it was hard to say whether or not it would change their minds. Eight months ago when the doctor told them there wasn't anything more that could be done for me, and sent me home, Momma and Daddy sat down with me and Mark and told us that the best we could do was to carry on as normally as possible. So far, they'd done just that, with a few exceptions that I wasn't supposed to notice.

"What are we going to do today?" Josie asked.

That was something about Josie. She pretty much left decisions up to me. I used to feel guilty, like I was getting my own way all the time, but then I realized she simply had no opinions of her own most of the time, and was only too glad to have someone decide things for her.

"Let's pack a lunch and just walk around and see what's happening," I suggested lamely. I hadn't really thought of any plans aside from getting away from the house for the day.

"Okay." She dressed hurriedly and we went downstairs, made some sandwiches, grabbed a few apples and juice, and headed out.

"What's he like?" she asked, as we neared the centre of town.

"Randy?" I thought for a minute. "He's kind of hard to describe, really. He seems smart, and likes the same kind of books I do. There's a feeling of mystery about him. From talking to him, you'd never think he'd be involved in anything like a robbery. I can't quite figure him out."

"I mean, what's he look like?"

"Average, I guess. Light hair and complexion. Kind of tall, and thin."

"So he's not cute or anything?" She seemed puzzled at this.

"Not really." I was suddenly tired of the questions. It struck me that the only thing important to her was the least important to me, and it made me feel sort of defensive.

"I could go up and see him, and give him a message for you."

I wondered why she wanted to see him, and more than that, why I felt at once that there was no way I wanted her doing it. I think it was partly because I sort of thought of him as someone I'd found on my own, and I didn't want to share him. But mostly it was because he'd said we'd be friends, and Josie might make him forget that he wished that. Boys went kind of gaga over Josie, and I worried that he'd do the same, and never notice that she had nothing in common with him.

Before I could answer, she had an idea. "Hey, I could take him up another book for you anytime you want. That way you'll be sure not to get caught for it."

I was torn between wanting to keep him to myself, and having this chance to send more books to him. I struggled with it for a moment, and then the noble side of me won over.

"Okay." I hesitated for a second. "Let's go get one now and you can drop it off for me."

So that's what we did. And I was glad afterward. When Josie came back, she had *Oliver Twist* in her hand. We decided to drop it off at my place before going anywhere else.

"So," I said, trying to sound more casual than I felt, "what did Randy have to say?"

"Not much," she shrugged. "He just said to thank you for the books and give this one back to you."

When we reached my house I took it up to my room, and that was when I noticed a piece of paper stuck inside. I slipped it out and opened it.

"Hey, what's that?" Josie asked, peering over my shoulder.

"A letter." I was excited, but tried to hide it. I really didn't want her to read it, although I didn't think I could wait to see it myself either.

"What's it say?" As I'd expected, she wanted to know. We didn't keep things from each other, and I couldn't think of any reason to hide this from her, so I read it out loud.

"Dear Kate," it began, "I want to tell you how much it means to me to have you sending me books while I'm in here. The distraction they provide is the only thing that makes being in this place bearable. The ones you've sent are as near to what I'd have picked for myself as I can imagine. I'm sorry you can't come up anymore, because it was really nice having someone to talk to, even for a few minutes. I also want you to know that I think you're a very special person. Your friend, Randy."

"That's nice," Josie said. She had already lost interest and was looking out the window to see if anyone happened to be passing on the street.

All of a sudden I didn't want Josie around anymore that day. That probably sounds mean, but it's the way I felt. It was one of those moments you get when you just want to be alone and enjoy a feeling and maybe figure things out. I also knew I wanted to write something back to Randy, but had no idea what to say.

"Josie," I said slowly, "I kind of feel tired all of a sudden. Maybe I should lay down for a bit. Would you mind if I did that — and maybe came over to your place again later?"

"Well, my mother said I could go with her to do some shopping for new school clothes this afternoon," Josie said slowly. "If you're not feeling good maybe I'll do that today, unless you're sure you're coming over soon." She paused, and then said hopefully, "I could call you when I get home."

I was glad that she had something else to do, and told her to go ahead and have a good time shopping. I felt kind of bad, because I knew she was feeling guilty about making other plans, and I didn't even want her around.

I flopped on my bed after she left and read Randy's letter over and over until I had it memorized. After a while I stuck it back between the pages of *Oliver Twist* and took out a pen and paper to write something to him. I sat in front of the blank paper for a long time, but no matter how hard I thought, I couldn't seem to write a word.

CHAPTER FIVE

Sunday started off like any other day. It amazes me when days that end up really important start off without so much as a hint that something out of the ordinary is going to happen.

Take the day I found out I had this tumour, for instance. I hadn't been really sick, just having these headaches. Momma had taken me to see why I was getting them, and the next thing I was in the hospital in the city with all kinds of weird tests being done. Doctor Stephens hadn't made it sound scary or anything, just said he had some concerns that he wanted to check out to be sure everything was okay.

It was a Tuesday when he finally told us everything wasn't okay. Actually, he didn't tell me at first. That kind of made me mad. I mean, it was me, my body they were talking about, and he took Momma and Daddy off somewhere and then they came back and told me. Momma was crying, and Daddy was looking the way he did when Grandpa died.

The doctor was behind them, but he stepped forward and sat on the edge of my bed and patted my arm.

"Kate," he said, after he'd cleared his throat a few times, "your parents feel that you have the right to know what's going on. You have a medical problem. Now, we'll do everything we can for you, and I believe we can lick this thing. But you have to fight it. You have to be strong and do exactly what I ask of you, even when it's not pleasant."

"Well, it's not like I'm going to die or anything, right?" I asked. It seemed like a stupid question to me at the time, and I'm not sure where it came from. It just kind of popped out. Momma cried harder. I think that's when I realized death might actually be a possibility.

"Not if we can help it," the doctor said, patting my arm again.

The medical problem turned out to be a brain tumour. I had radiation and chemotherapy for it, and the doctor told me it had shrunk but it was still there. Some kinds of brain tumours can be operated on, but not mine. When they finished with my chemo I felt like I'd been through an old wringer washer like the one Grandma used to have. Doctor Stephens sat down with us and told us they had bought me time and that was all that could be done.

They bought me time! I nearly laughed when he said that. I'd been so sick, so fed up with the awful taste of metal in my mouth, the heat running through my veins, the way my body let me know that it didn't appreciate what was being done to it. I pretty much felt that if anyone had bought me time, it was me.

And you know what else? I didn't want to pay that price for time again. No way. I told Momma that, no matter what, I wasn't going to take any more treatments. It just wasn't worth it, if they couldn't save me. I'd have gone through it ten more times to live, but I wasn't going to live. I was just going to be sick and feel rotten for the sake of a few months or whatever.

Well, there, I've wandered off again. I was telling you about Sunday, and how it started off normally and turned into a pretty neat day.

We went to church in the morning, like we did every Sunday. Pastor Anders was talking about faith and how it works inside us to make God real in the way we live. I like his preaching. He never goes on with big words and grand sounds and gestures the way some preachers do. He talks like it matters to him that we understand.

Mrs. Standing sang a song that morning too. She has a nice voice, but I always want to laugh when she sings in front of the church. No matter what song she sings, she gets tears in her eyes and this look on her face like she's glimpsed glory and is there to show it to us. I watch her singing with the congregation lots of times to see if she's moved that way when she's not up in front of the whole church, and I've never seen any evidence of it yet. She just sings like a regular person then, no matter how inspiring the song is. Sometimes she even looks bored.

I'd mentioned this to Mark one time, and ever since he always nudges me when Mrs. Standing is singing. Momma catches him at it every time he nudges me in church, and asks us on the way home if we'd like to share our little secret. I think adults take the whole church thing too seriously. It's not like I don't believe in God, because I do. But it seems to me there's too much importance put on this one day when everyone sits and feels religious and then goes home and goes about things just the same as always. I think God should be a constant thing in your heart.

I like to talk to God just at any old time. I tell Him how I'm feeling about lots of things, and let Him know that I appreciate lots of stuff, but for some odd reason I almost never get to feeling real close and personal that way when I'm in church. Funny, huh?

Well, anyway, after church we were invited to lunch at the Baxters' house. Mr. and Mrs. Baxter are nice, but I don't much like their kids. They have twins, a boy and a girl, who are a couple of years younger than me.

Someone told them once that some twins can understand each other's thoughts without talking, which strikes me as nonsense. But they took it as gospel, and ever since, they'll try to impress people by staring at each other and letting on that they know what each other is thinking.

It's not something you can actually prove as being wrong. For example, Vicki will say, "Ricky is thinking about such and such," and Ricky will agree that that's exactly what he was thinking. It's downright boring, not to mention annoying.

They've turned it into some sort of parlour trick that they force on anyone unlucky enough to be trapped in their presence, which Mark and I pretty much were this day. It went on for a good hour before lunch was ready, and by then I wanted to gag more than I wanted to eat.

After lunch I volunteered to help with the dishes so I wouldn't have to be subjected to any more of the twins, and then we were ready to leave.

On the way home Momma was saying what a nice lunch it was and what nice people the Baxters are and the general kind of thing she says when we've left someone's place after a visit. I was looking out the window, not paying too much mind to anything at all, just sort of floating along in that vague area a person gets in when they hear what's being said around them but aren't really letting any of it take hold.

I hadn't even noticed we were near the jail until Momma's tone changed. It was the change of tone that brought my attention around more than the words, although the words would have wormed their way in after a few minutes.

"Who could this be?" Momma said. "Why, Orville, that poor woman is crying."

I swung my eyes around and got things back in focus in time to see us pass a woman leaning on an old, beat-up-looking car. She was crying all right, and sort of clutching at the door of the car.

"Orville!" Momma cried, as though he had done some dreadful thing and caused this woman's grief. "You stop the car and back up this very minute. That poor woman is in distress. How *could* you just pass by that way?"

Daddy muttered something about such a thing as minding your own business, but he stopped the car and backed up just like Momma said. We no sooner got beside the woman than Momma was out and at her side. We could all hear the conversation that went on between them, since it was hot and all the windows were down on our car.

"Excuse me, ma'am," Momma said very gently, "we couldn't but notice that you were upset. Is there anything we can do to help?"

The woman just cried harder, turning her face toward Momma with this awful heartbroken look. She was small, and she looked as frail as anyone I'd ever seen. For the first time I understood what a person meant when they described someone as mousy looking. This woman was definitely mousy looking, with a colourless, pointed kind of face and frightened eyes.

Momma put her hand on one tiny shoulder. "There, there," she said in the kindest of tones, "Won't you come along with us and have a cup of tea? You look like you need to rest for a bit."

There was a moment of indecision on the woman's face before she nodded and whispered, "Thank you." Momma took her arm and led her over to our car, opening the front passenger door for her. She shook her head no and insisted that she would ride in the back. Momma gave in quickly with a satisfied look on her face. I knew that she felt it was right to offer the woman her seat, but also right for the offer to be refused. Little things like that confirm a person's character for Momma.

Mark squeezed over beside me to make room in the back seat. The back of his hand rested hot against the back of mine, but I didn't move away even though I don't like hot hands against me. I knew it made him feel uncomfortable that a stranger was crammed in there with us, and he needed that little sense of closeness to me.

"We just live a few minutes away," Momma was saying. The woman hiccupped and hunted in her purse, which was a cheap vinyl type with a tear along one edge, until she found a tissue. She dabbed her eyes and nose with it and then scrunched it up in a soggy ball in her hand all the rest of the drive. She was breathing in little half-sobbing gulps like Mark used to when he was small and was settling after a major upset.

As we drove Momma introduced us all, and the woman told us her name was Irene Nichols.

When we got to the house Mrs. Nichols' face changed again. She looked like she wished she hadn't come. Momma didn't seem to notice that, and just whisked her right along into the living room.

"Kate, dear, you entertain our guest while I make some tea," she said cheerily, as though this was a normal social call. Then off she went to the kitchen leaving me standing there.

I sat down on the couch and looked across to the chair where Mrs. Nichols sat — perched on the edge of her seat and looking as though she'd like the earth to divide and swallow her whole. She kept her eyes down, as if there was something on her lap that she couldn't tear her attention from.

"It sure has been warm," I said at last, hating that it was all I could think of.

She looked up, startled, as though just realizing I was in the room, and her eyes met mine. With a shock, I recognized them.

"You're Randy's mother!" I said. The mention of his name brought the first real sign of life into her that I'd seen. She leaned forward, peering at me with interest.

"How do you know my boy?" she asked.

"Well now, here's a nice cup of tea for you," Momma's voice broke in. She followed a tray holding tea and cupcakes into the room, and sat it down on what she always called the occasional table. I never understood why it was called that, since it's a table all the time.

Mrs. Nichols' eyes were still on me with their question. I wished Momma hadn't come back in so soon.

"I took some meals up to him," I said finally. "He's a very nice boy."

"A woman never had a better son." She paused for a moment, during which time Momma's face went from puzzled to understanding, with surprise mixed in the whole time.

"It must sound strange to hear that," she continued, "considering what he's just done. But it's still true. Randy has never given me a minute of trouble before, and it was only circumstance that led him to do what he did. I don't expect people who don't know him to understand that, but if they knew the whole story they'd not be harsh in their judgement of him."

"Have you come to bail him out?" I asked, knowing as soon as the words were out of my mouth that it was the wrong thing to say. I have a habit of saying things and then considering the wisdom of them afterward. Daddy tells me all the time to think before I speak, but his advice never pops into my head at the right moment.

A flood of tears followed my question. Every time she seemed to be struggling to stop crying, a fresh wave of emotion would wash over her and it would start again.

It was some time before she could control herself enough to talk, and when she did her words were accompanied by hiccups and sniffles.

"Bail him out?" she asked sadly. "I wish with my whole heart that I could. It just tears me up inside to see him locked in that room. My Randy, so free spirited. He loves the outdoors you know, practically lives outside all summer long. But I'm afraid it's impossible."

At this point she drew a deep breath, and there was a look on her face like she was making a decision. When she began to speak again, her face had cleared, and I knew she had decided to tell us the whole story.

"I married Randy's father against my parents' wishes," she said quietly. "It seems a lifetime ago now. My mother and father felt he was wild, no good. All I saw was a dashing young man full of excitement."

She straightened her shoulders and lifted her head. "I came from a good home, but my parents were strict and unforgiving. After I married Jake they never spoke to me again, right until the day they died. Oh, I've paid for my mistake and paid dearly. Jake isn't really a bad man, just weak. Funny how the things that seemed to make him strong in my eyes when we met proved to be weaknesses. He never took lip from anyone, but that cost him a number of jobs until finally no one would hire him. He took to drinking too much, being gone for days and weeks at a time. I know it's because he felt like a failure and couldn't face us."

Momma pressed a cup of tea into her hands.

"When my mother died, two years after my father had passed on, I got a surprise. They had left the farm to me! I guess it was their way of saying I was finally forgiven. We moved in and tried to work the land, but it was hard. Jake got discouraged and went back to his old ways again. Randy did what he could, but he was in school and there was only so much time he could spend helping me. We were forced to take out a mortgage on the farm.

"Things went from bad to worse. Creditors everywhere, no money to pay them. The crops were small and didn't yield much. Two months ago the bank man came over and told me we had sixty days to come up with four thousand dollars or they would be forced to foreclose. I know that's what drove Randy to do such a desperate thing. He was just trying to get money somehow to help me save the farm."

Momma cleared her throat the way she does when she's trying not to cry. "How much longer do you have before they take the farm?" she asked after a moment.

"They took it today." Her tiny hands spread out in front of her as she said this, almost in apology for having to tell us yet another piece of bad news. "I'm on my way to my cousin's house. She lives about eight hundred miles away from here, and I just had to see my boy before I left. When this is all over with, he can join me there and we'll find some way to get a place of our own."

I was thinking about the old car we'd found her beside, and wondering how on earth it was going to make a trip of eight hundred miles. I was also thinking that I could have had years of disappointment and sorrow like Mrs. Nichols, and that dying young isn't necessarily a terrible thing.

"You look so tired," Momma was saying. "Why don't you rest a while. Have dinner with us and stay the night. Tomorrow will be soon enough to start out on your journey. And you can see your boy again before you go."

"I *am* terribly tired," Mrs. Nichols said. "I'd be very grateful to take you up on your offer. You've all been so kind, I hardly know what to say."

Mrs. Nichols stayed that night, and the next few nights too. Word got around, and by the third day she was with us the town was thinking of Randy in a new light.

CHAPTER SIX

Needless to say, my folks took a different approach to the idea of me seeing Randy after Mrs. Nichols happened into our lives. It seemed pointless to mention that if they'd trusted my judgement, instead of waiting to have it confirmed by an adult, we could have avoided a lot of hard feelings.

Other things were happening too, things that were more important than my being able to talk to Randy again. For one thing, Mrs. Nichols stayed on in Farrago.

That came about on Wednesday afternoon. I was sitting out on the front porch, watching Mark play with his toy soldiers, when Mrs. Wickholm, whom you'll recall as being the dentist's wife, came up the walk.

"Good afternoon, Kate," she greeted me, with the air of a grand lady taking time to speak to a peasant.

"Good afternoon, Mrs. Wickholm," I said back, trying hard for the same air, but succeeding only in sounding silly and, if the look she gave me was any indication, impertinent. Well, I guess the goal there was impertinence if one must be completely honest about these things.

"I've come to see Mrs. Nichols," she announced, looking about as though the very words from her mouth ought to make Mrs. Nichols appear.

"I'll fetch her, ma'am," I said, glad for the excuse to leave.

Momma and Mrs. Nichols were in the kitchen, talking and peeling apples for a pie. In the few days she'd been with us, she'd lost some of the scared look on her face.

"Excuse me," I said first off. For some reason I always seemed to remember my best manners around Mrs. Nichols. "Momma, Mrs. Wickholm is here to see Mrs. Nichols."

Momma scowled but covered it up quick. I figured she was thinking that a visit from Mrs. Wickholm could be a long and tedious event, and the pie would never get made in time for supper. But she stood, washed her hands in the sink, and went into the parlour with Mrs. Nichols right behind her.

I was curious, and would have followed the women, just on the off chance that I wouldn't get sent away. That's what usually happens when adults are visiting at our house. But at that very moment Josie appeared at the door, wanting me to go for a walk. I wasn't in a walking mood, but since I still felt guilty about getting rid of her the other day, I went.

Josie had a funny look about her this day. It was the kind of look she gets when she has something to tell me, but is waiting for just the right moment for it. We walked for a while — pretty much in silence at first — and I was losing patience by the time she finally spoke.

"I have something to tell you," she whispered, although there was no one around to hear her.

"I figured," I said.

She looked at me sideways. I think she was looking for a sign of interest, and I felt ashamed. It's not much fun to tell news to someone who doesn't appear to care if they hear it.

I stopped walking and turned to face her. "Well, what is it?" I asked as eagerly as I could. Truth be told I've had a hard time focussing on things lately. Mostly I seem to be lost in my own thoughts with only a vague awareness of what's happening around me.

"Parker Jamison kissed me!" she said, and immediately started to giggle.

"Porker?" I asked incredulously. I guess it was rude, but he'd been short and fat all through grade school, and now that he'd slimmed down and gotten taller it was hard to think of him in new terms.

"Parker," she snapped, as her colour got a little higher than usual. "And he's very nice."

It occurred to me that this was the way it should be for Josie's first kiss. After all, they'd both been ridiculed a lot. If she'd gone and kissed one of the boys who was always popular, it would have been a sort of betrayal, but with Parker, it was just right.

I apologized for calling him Porker, and tried to explain that I hadn't meant anything bad by it. I even said he was cute now, which isn't completely true, although he's not ugly or anything.

"What was it like?" I asked. This wasn't a put-on of interest either. I really wanted to know.

She smiled with a far-away, dreamy look on her face. Josie gets this look about a lot of so-called romantic things, and one can never tell if it's the event that's bringing it about, or just her idea of the event.

After a minute she said, "It was sort of magical," in a hushed tone.

"Magical?" I wanted to laugh, but managed not to. I've tried to imagine what it would be like to have a boy kiss me, and magical never entered my thoughts. After all, my parents and brother have kissed me lots of times, and it can't be that different, except that the pair of lips are new to you. This was clearly Josie's interpretation more than actual fact.

"Yes," she sighed. "We were sitting on the picnic table in the backyard. He asked me if he could kiss me, and when I said yes he leaned over and it was the most wonderful thing."

I guess it's good manners for a boy to ask a girl if he can kiss her, but something about that seems ridiculous to me. I thought if I were ever to get kissed (not that it seemed likely to happen) I wouldn't want to be asked first.

"Why are you looking like that?" Josie was asking.

"I'm not looking like anything," I denied, knowing full well I was.

"You are too. You look like you just find the whole thing funny. I'd never have told you at all if I'd known you were going to make fun of me."

"Honest, Josie, I'm not making fun of you. I guess I just can't quite picture it, that's all."

"Well, whatever picture of it you have is wrong," she snapped. "It's plain from the look on your face that you think the whole thing is amusing."

She looked so indignant, standing there with her hands on her hips and her mouth pursed in a little pucker of disapproval. For some reason, when I most needed to be serious and fix things between us, it struck me that maybe she'd pursed her mouth up that way when Parker kissed her.

The thought of that was too much for me, Josie's mouth in this strange little pinched look, Parker's probably the same, the two of them likely as red as beets, kissing, and then having the event described as magical.

I burst out laughing. It was a terrible thing to do, but it was no excuse for what she said to me then.

"You're jealous, Kate Benchworth," she said in what was partly a wail and partly a yell. "You're jealous because I've been kissed and you're never going to be kissed. Ever."

Her words sort of hung in the air between us. We stood looking at each other while they sank in. Sometimes words do that, they get in your head and take up a place there and grow.

It was almost comical, the horrified expression that came over her face. You'd have thought I was the one who'd said it to her instead of the other way around.

The worst things was, we both knew it was true. Boys tended to avoid girls who were fourteen and dying, with their hair sticking up in silly-looking spikes. Besides that, I hadn't yet really begun to, um, grow much, although Momma had politely insisted I needed a training bra and brought home a truly awful pink lacy one some months back. I never told her I hated it, sitting in my dresser drawer, peeking out all feminine and healthy looking.

I drew myself up (I don't much like this expression, but it does fit what I'm trying to describe here) and gave Josie what I hoped was an icy look before turning and walking deliberately away. Her voice behind me, all broken, calling my name, added to my satisfaction. I didn't turn or answer her, and as I got further away I heard her start crying outright.

I could have gone back right then, and we might have hugged and made up, but I didn't. I kept myself from it by pushing aside the wrong I'd done, and concentrating on the wrong she'd done, which I suspect is generally the way people make the most of this sort of thing.

I didn't feel like going right home, even though I was curious to find out what Mrs. Wickholm had come to see Randy's mother about. And I didn't feel like being around anyone, although I considered going to see Randy for a bit. It seemed that I needed to be alone to settle the whole thing in my mind, so I turned off the street near Wickett's Corner and took the path into the woods.

This isn't my favourite part of the woods around Farrago, but it suited me this day. I usually prefer to take smaller paths that are less known and walked, rather than the trail that lovers favour. It passes a freshwater spring in the side of the hill, though, and when I need something outside myself to find a sense of peace, it helps.

I sat there for a while, looking at the black stones that line the pool under the spring. They look almost like black pearls, all worn from the years of water running over them. Sometimes I take one out and hold it in my hand, and feel the cold smoothness. But I always put them back before they dry out, because the beauty gets lost when they dry, and then they're just like any stone you might find along the road. It takes the water and the stones together, being right where they are, to give them that certain meaning.

I thought about this as I sat there, how things have a certain place in the world, and how if you disturb the order, they don't do what they're meant to. I wondered what my place in the world was, if I was in it or if something had moved me around and left me without meaning. It's hard to find meaning in your life at the best of times, but when you know you just have a short space left to fill, it's even harder.

It was at that moment that I decided to write my story down, and leave it behind me when I was gone. The more I thought about it, the more it seemed that was the right place for me to be, in words somewhere on paper. Not that I expect anyone will ever read this, but, well, you never know.

CHAPTER SEVEN

That night at dinner I found out what Mrs. Wickholm had wanted. Momma was maddeningly slow at getting around to the news, even though I'd hinted after it three or four times. It's not considered polite in our house for kids to come right out and ask about "adult business" so I couldn't go about it directly.

"So, Irene, you'll be leaving us on Friday," she said, pausing with her fork in the air, which Mark and I are not allowed to do. "We'll surely miss having you here."

Mrs. Nichols smiled, a rare occurrence for her. "I can never thank you enough for all you've done," she said quietly. I noticed that when Mrs. Nichols spoke, there was often something almost totally unemotional about it. I wondered if she was losing the ability to feel, or the courage.

"Where you going?" Mark asked. I was glad he asked, even though Daddy gave him The Look for it.

"I'm going to work for Mrs. Wickholm," Mrs. Nichols answered. A small pause slid by, and then with a twinkle in her eyes she added, "She came this afternoon to offer me a domestic position."

I was pleased to hear her say that in just the way she did. It told me that she had a sense of humour, which I hadn't suspected until that very moment. It was a comfort in a way. I'd hate to think that a person would have lived the hard life she had without being able to laugh every once in a while.

And I could picture it too, no problem at all. Mrs. Wickholm sitting up straight with her regal air, feeling like the saviour of the situation and using the words "domestic position" as though she was born with them in her mouth, and hadn't grown up on a farm with six other children, collecting eggs and shovelling manure out of the barn.

Mark had missed The Look. "What's that?" he asked.

"Children ought not to be putting their noses where they don't belong," Daddy said sternly. Of course it was easy for him to decide that. He'd already been filled in on the news. It's curious how parents want to know all about things, but act like it's some kind of outrage if their children show any interest.

"Yes, sir," Mark said, at the same time that Mrs. Nichols informed him it was a job as a housekeeper.

Tue Jun 17-08 12:03A
Inv: 202501 M Qu

Qty.	Price Disc	Total Tax

7818530_140 Kate
1   12.99   12.99 1

	Subtotal	12.99
	Tax GST	0.65
Items	1 Total	13.64
	Cash	20.00
	Change Due	6.36

Thank You

Have A Great Day

And that was how it came about that Mrs. Nichols stayed on in Farrago.

I went up to see Randy the next morning. Mrs. Nichols usually went up every afternoon and evening, and I didn't feel right about going there when she was with him. I figured they'd want privacy to talk.

"Hey! Kate," he said, as soon as he saw me. He got a big smile on his face, and it made a warm happy feeling spring up inside me.

"Howdy," I said, though I don't know where such a corny word came from. Fact is, I felt kind of corny all of a sudden.

For a minute we stood smiling at each other. I guessed he was pretty lonely and was glad for any company at all, but inside I was hoping a tiny bit of his smile was because he liked me.

"I sure am glad to see you, Kate," he said after a minute. "I was wondering if you'd be up soon."

My heart gave the queerest little leap when he said that. And I was suddenly horribly conscious that my hair was as short as a boy's and that I was no raving beauty by any means. It hadn't mattered to me much before, what with everything else going on in my life, but now it mattered a lot.

"Well, how've you been?" I asked finally.

"I'm doing okay," he said. "My mother told me what your folks have done for her, and I wish you'd tell them that I sure appreciate it."

"I'll tell them," I nodded. "How are your books holding out? I meant to bring a couple more but Momma called me as I was going out and I set them on the table in the hallway and forgot to get them again when I went out the door."

"I'm good for another night," he answered. "I do most of my reading at night when things are quiet. In the daytime I watch out the window a little and wonder about the people I see passing by. I can't see too much close by, what with the back fence and all, but there's a good view through the vacant lot over in the next street."

Remembering, he added, "This morning quite early I saw your friend, the one you sent some books up with once. I'm sorry, but I don't recall her name."

"Josie," I said, glad that he'd forgotten it and suffering only the tiniest twinge of guilt for my disloyalty.

"Is she your best friend?"

"We've been best friends for years," I said, "but we had a fight the other day." I suddenly found myself telling him all about the incident that had taken place between us such a short time ago.

"I don't know what to do about it now," I ended. I felt miserable for the telling, as if it had just happened as I was speaking.

Randy had listened without interrupting as I spoke, and when I was through he sat quietly for a bit before saying anything.

"I guess going to someone who's wronged us in some way is a hard thing," he spoke at last, "especially if we've been wrong too. That's the hardest part. Both sides tend to want the other person to come to them, therefore proving that they were a little bit *more* wrong. It's a tough one."

I thought on this for a moment.

"Well then, what do you think I should do?" I asked.

"I guess if I wanted to patch things up with someone, I'd just call them up as if nothing happened and ask them over or something. I'd just pretty much ignore the whole thing and go on."

"But guys are different from girls," I explained, surprised that he didn't know it. "Girls like to settle a thing, talk it out and stuff." I felt very wise. "It's because of a thing called social conditioning."

"Now where'd you go and hear this?" Randy asked. He was on the verge of laughing, and I felt at once foolish and angry.

"I'll have you know I read it in a book," I said indignantly. "It explained about how women need to deal with emotional things 'cause they've been raised to nurture. Men aren't. They're taught to hide their emotions to prove that they're strong, so they just ignore a lot of that kind of thing."

"Oh, I see," Randy said, smirking.

I was enraged. "Thank you so much for showing respect for my views," I said, clipping my words.

"Those aren't your views at all," he said mildly. "They're just something you read and decided to take on as your own. That's different than believing a thing because you came into it from your own thoughts."

"Well, excuse me, Mr. Deep Thinker," I snapped. "I learned two plus two makes four from a book as well. I suppose I should just throw that aside since I didn't come into it from my own thoughts."

"That's math. It's a different thing. You're talking about human behaviour, and there are as many theories on that as people who've written about it."

"So you automatically decide that the book I read is wrong?" I asked none too sweetly.

"The book you read might be as right as rain," he answered. "But it's kind of like politics. Most people grow up and vote for the party their folks support in elections, just because they've been told to. They don't often look any further into it and make up their own mind. I'm just saying you should study different points of view before you go around saying a thing is right. If you don't, you're committing yourself to accepting someone else's ideas without really thinking them through and looking at other sides. And you're far too smart for that."

"You think I'm smart?" I asked, pleased and ready to forgive the whole argument.

"As a whip," he answered, and then with a teasing look he added, "but that's just my opinion. Get some others before you make a firm decision on the matter."

I laughed with him on that. "I don't need any others," I said, tossing my head. "I knew it already from years of st— umm, (I'd been about to say 'study' but switched in mid-word) consideration."

"That's my girl," he rejoined.

My heart like to stopped at those words. My girl. Randy had called me his girl! Oh, I knew down inside he didn't actually mean it like that, but it was enough to make me blush as red as an overripe cherry. I hoped like heck that he'd think the blush was from arguing and not suspect how I was feeling. I wasn't quite sure if I suspected it in all honesty my own self.

"I'll say one thing," Randy blurted out suddenly. "Your friend was sure wrong about you not getting kissed. Before you know it boys will be lining up waiting for a chance to kiss you, Kate."

This statement surprised me and took my breath and words all in one. Then I remembered that Randy didn't know I was dying, and that his prediction didn't take that into account. I guess if ever there was a moment I should have told him, it would have been then, but I let it pass for reasons I didn't quite understand myself.

Instead, I said, "Well, I'm not interested in kissing any silly old boys anyway, so that hardly matters."

"Isn't there even one nice boy anywhere in Farrago that you'd secretly like to kiss?" Randy asked.

"No. And even if there were," I said, "I sure wouldn't feel inclined to discuss it with you."

"I guess that a girl like you would need someone pretty special to catch her interest." This was said in a contemplative way, as though not exactly addressed to me.

I didn't know what to say to that, so I stayed quiet, trying to sort out all the wild things rushing around in my insides. It was like some crazy virus had taken hold and was tearing here and there, dancing and tromping out of control.

"It's true." Randy's voice broke through my thoughts. "You're not like any girl I've ever met. Most of 'em are always giggling and worrying about their makeup and hair and stuff and wouldn't know what to do with a serious thought if it hit them over the head."

I looked up at him then and his eyes were full on me. I looked right into them for just a few seconds and felt like I might suffocate and die right there and then on the floor of the Farrago Police Station.

For the first time in my life, or at least that I could remember, words betrayed me by hiding off somewhere beyond my reach.

Chapter EIGHT

I guess no one had given a whole lot of thought to Mr. Nichols at this point in time. Well, I suppose Mrs. Nichols had, but for the rest of the town he was pretty much non-existent. It didn't take long for that to change when he made an appearance Thursday night.

I hadn't been feeling well all day. It's not that I have a lot of pain or anything. I'm fortunate that way, because a lot of people suffer a whole lot and spend their last months in misery. I just get so that I can hardly move off the bed at times, but it's more a tired, weak feeling than anything else.

Momma brought a tray in for me at suppertime. I can count on her to make my favourite foods when I'm down like that, and I appreciate it even though I don't feel much like eating. I do my best, though, so that she'll feel the effort was worth it.

She sat down beside the bed and put her hand on my forehead. I smiled up at her, which was a mistake because she got all full of tears then and had an awful time keeping them inside.

"I think it'd be okay for you to cry if you feel like it, Momma," I said. "I know you want to be strong for me, but I realize this is hard on you. You should be able to let it out sometimes."

For some reason, I had the idea that Momma just went through from day to day keeping it all in. What she said next took me by surprise.

"Kate, my child," she began with a tremble in her voice, "there are times when I think I can't have any more tears left in me, that I must surely have spilled enough for four lifetimes. Right now, many of them are for what you're facing and how it must feel for you. But some of them are selfish, because you're my daughter and I love you and I never thought I'd have to face losing you. It doesn't seem natural somehow, for a child to go before the parents."

Regaining some of her composure, she cleared her throat and went on. "These past months I've struggled to accept what's coming. I know that the good Lord is in control, and this must be His will, even though we may never understand it this side of glory. I do believe that the separation between us is only a temporary thing, that someday we'll be united again. This is the only thing that gives me strength, and I pray will continue to give me strength in time to come."

Something burst in me at that moment, a flood of emotion that must have been there all along and been shoved down all the while I'd known I was going to die. Somehow it became more real with my mother's words. She had accepted it, and learned to deal with it in a way I never had. I'd just had it in me in a vague sort of way, without truly facing it.

"I'm going to die," I wailed, sobbing and shaking as though the news had just been delivered. "I'm only fourteen and I'm going to die."

Momma held me against her, mixing her tears with mine and not shushing me as she used to when I cried. I clung to her long after my tears were spent. An hour passed, and then another. At some time Daddy came to the doorway, paused, said, "I'll see to getting supper on the table, Lillian," and disappeared.

Finally exhaustion overtook me and I slept. When I woke it was dark, but a light burned in the hallway, illuminating my room. I saw that Momma had placed a basket with fruit, cheese, and crackers on my bedside table. Feeling hungry, I sat up to eat.

I worked my way through an apple and a hunk of gouda cheese, slicing a piece of each and putting them together, which is my favourite way to eat an apple.

While I ate I noted with surprise that I actually felt pretty good. The sadness had spent itself, and left me feeling stronger. It was as though having truly realized my situation, I could move forward. There was a strange sense of relief, as though the worst had been faced and hadn't beat me. Knowing I was dying and actually accepting it were two different things. There was nothing to fear in the dying itself now that the idea of it had settled in me.

I slipped out of bed and headed for the bathroom on tiptoe so as not to disturb anyone. I'd just finished in there and was about to go back to my room when the quiet of the night was broken by some sort of commotion that came from the veranda.

Hurrying to the end of the hall, I peered out the window that overlooked the front of the house just in time to see our metal garbage can roll to a rest against the railing. At the same time I heard Momma saying, "Orville, wake up! There's a noise downstairs."

Daddy came from their room pulling his bathrobe closed and trying to focus his way down the hall. He saw me standing at the window and stopped with a confused look on his face.

"Something knocked over the garbage can," I whispered.

"Probably dogs," Daddy grumbled, looking annoyed that his sleep had been disturbed for this.

I smushed my nose up against the windowpane and tried to see if there were any signs of dogs out there. What I saw instead surprised me so much that I almost jumped back. A man had staggered into my view, waving his arm toward the upended garbage can as though it had rolled there against his express wishes and needed chastisement. He took a step backward, landed against the front railing, and went up and over into the rosebushes.

A yell rose from him, prompting Daddy to join me at the window posthaste, now completely awake.

"What the heck?" he sputtered. We watched together as the man momentarily flopped around like a fish on a beach, after which he disentangled himself from the bushes, taking a good bunch of Momma's roses off in the process. He got to his feet after an unsuccessful first attempt in which he tried to pull himself up by grasping onto a rose bush, an effort that brought a fresh although blurry yell from him.

Daddy was just turning to head down the stairs when the man called out his first intelligible word.

"Ire-ene!" It had the sound of a young calf bawling.

The lights were going on in the houses around us, faces appearing with hands cupped around them to block out the lights they'd just turned on. Our front-yard drama was sure to be news all over town at the first sign of morning.

"Ire-ene." This time clearer, the voice had become insistent.

I made a futile attempt to follow Daddy as he went downstairs, stepping back when he turned and told me to stay put.

"In fact," he added, "you'd better go back to your room."

Just then Mrs. Nichols came from the downstairs guest room and down the hall with a look on her face that said "here we go again" just as clear as any words I've ever heard spoken.

"I'm real sorry," she said to Daddy. "I'll see to it."

"You'd better not go out there," Daddy cautioned. "He seems to be, uh, under the weather."

Mrs. Nichols' hand fluttered out in a wave that dismissed Daddy's objection and she went out the front door and stood facing her husband. I hurried back to the window upstairs so as to have a good vantage point. At first I couldn't make out what they were saying, but sliding the window open an inch took care of that.

"Got nuthin leff adall," Mr. Nichols blubbered.

"You just get yourself on out of here before these good people call the police, which they have every right to do," she answered him.

"I ain't scared uh no coppers," he assured her, pulling himself up taller. A rose petal drifted from his hair down over his face, and he blew it off as if it were the police in question and he was making his point.

"Anyhow," he added, with a flash of clarity, "if they lock me up, I'll see muh boy."

This did not seem to have occurred to Mrs. Nichols, and her face changed to near panic at the thought.

"Haven't you brought enough grief to Randy and me?" she asked bitterly. "If there was one decent bone in your body you'd leave right now like I'm asking and never trouble us again."

"I never meant tuh bring nobody no grief," Mr. Nichols said, back to blubbering. "I juss had a run o' bad luck izall."

"Jake Nichols, you listen to me here and now and you listen up good. I've been employed by a lady in this town and intend to stay here until I know what's going to happen to my son. After he's free again, I'm going to take him away from here and make a life for us. You aren't going to be part of that life. Not ever again. I've had it with you. Do you hear me?"

"Nobody cares about me," Mr. Nichols sobbed outright.

Mrs. Nichols' face was set in something between a frown and a grimace. She looked at him without pity, and then turned and walked slowly up the veranda steps.

"No, nobody does. Not anymore," she said. She stopped, swung suddenly around to face him again, and in a clear, calm voice she told him that if he ever bothered her or Randy again, she would kill him.

Well, sir! I'd have been tempted to laugh right out, hearing something like that from this bit of a woman to the big, hulking man swaying on our lawn, except for the look on her face and the way the words came out of her.

Mr. Nichols stared after her as she went inside, closing the door behind her without so much as a backward glance. His mouth opened and closed several times, but not a sound came out. He seemed to shrink into himself then.

As if his eyes were magnetically drawn, Mr. Nichols looked up to the window and saw me. He raised a hand in a pleading way and called out to me.

"You tell Irene that I ain't going to trouble her or the boy no more," he said. "But I'm agonna change. She'll see. I'm agonna make sumthin of meself. And when I do, I'll be back and she'll be glad to have me."

With that he stumbled off down the driveway and in a few minutes had disappeared up the road out of sight.

The story got told around the next day all right, and with it were the added touches that kind of story usually enjoys. We heard later in the day that Mr. Nichols had been found sleeping on a bench on Queen Street in the early hours of the morning.

The person who happened on him was none other than Maryanne Richards, and the news that she was out walking was almost as big as the story about Randy's father. Apparently she had seen him and called the police when she got home to tell them there was a vagrant to be tended to.

Officer Tremblay had taken the call and logged it in his book, being new in town, a rookie and conscientious. When Officer Peterson read the entry he asked him over and over if he was sure about the name. Finally, certain there was a mistake, he telephoned Maryanne herself.

"She said yes it was her," he said later. "I told her, but Maryanne, you haven't left your house in years."

"Well, I guess I must have," he reported her as answering, "else I couldn't have seen that bum on the bench, now could I?"

Even Officer Peterson couldn't argue with that kind of logic.

CHAPTER NINE

The morning after Mr. Nichols' visit in our rose-bushes I went down to the river to turn things over in my head. It's a good place to do that, especially when the water is calm, which it was this day.

It seemed the past few weeks had given me more to think about than a person usually has to figure out in a year, what with meeting Randy, having a fight with Josie, Randy's mom coming to town, and then his father showing up. But strangely enough, the thing most on my mind was none of those things. It was Maryanne Richards.

I guess I'd never given much thought to her before, just accepted that she was a recluse who had nothing to do with my life and little to do with the town aside from gossip value when there wasn't much else to talk about. Women brought the subject of Maryanne up in the same way that men kept talking over old sport events. They went over the fine points of what *had* happened and wasted talk making suggestions about what *could* have happened to make the ending different.

That was where it always ended in talk of Maryanne. I'd never thought of it before, but this day I realized it was a lot different than a sports game that had a fixed ending to it. That was done and nothing could undo or change it, but when you're talking about a human being who lives right in your town, isn't there a chance that something could change the outcome for that person?

Everyone spoke of Maryanne as if her way of life was a permanent and fixed thing. I'd often heard old ladies say that she'd never come out of her house until they carried her in a pine box. Well, she'd fooled them. She'd been out after all. I wondered if it was the first time she'd taken a walk or if maybe she regularly slipped out in the early morning before the town was awake.

It was just possible that Maryanne Richards had secrets locked up in that house with her, secrets of feeling and doing. If she did, I was keen to find them out. She'd suddenly become someone of interest to me.

Still, it didn't seem likely that there was any way I could find any of these things out. I felt a sense of advance regret for the plan forming in my mind because the chance of success was so small it hardly even counted. Nevertheless, I was going to try to talk to her.

A person couldn't just walk up and knock on her door. She never let anyone in, not even the boys who delivered her groceries. They knew to sit them on the step, ring the doorbell, and leave.

I could have called her on the phone, but, from what I'd heard, people who'd tried that over the years hadn't met with any success. She just cut them right off. Besides, what would I say?

I went home after giving it a little more thought, took a clean white sheet of paper, and wrote in neat little letters right in the centre of the page:

> Miss Kate Benchworth
> requests the pleasure
> of accompanying
> Mrs. Maryanne Richards
> on her next early morning stroll

I put my address and phone number down in the right-hand corner of the page, slipped it into an envelope, and mailed it off right away before I could change my mind.

There have been lots of times in my life that I've started to do something and then, after waiting and thinking it through, abandoned the plan altogether. Some of them I'm pretty sure were best left undone, but others have come back to haunt me and mocked my lack of courage.

I took a walk down near Josie's house then, hoping to run into her casually on the street, but there was no sign of her anywhere. I'd given up and was heading back home when I spied her youngest brother, Reggie, coming toward me.

"Hi, Kate!" he called, waving. "You lookin' for Josie?"

"No, I'm looking for the Manse Monster," I said. That was a story Josie and I had made up to frighten him once, but instead of getting scared he'd delightedly begged for more and more gory details until we were exhausted from the effort and bored with the whole thing.

"Yeah?" he smiled. "Well, he ain't here. He went over to your place to hide under your bed. He's going to come crawling out when you're sleeping and leave black slime all over you."

"That can't be true," I told him. "The Manse Monster only likes little boys, just about your size. He likes 'em for breakfast especially." I caught him quick under his arms and tickled his tummy until he fell laughing to the ground.

"Having fun?"

I swung around at the voice and stood facing Josie's boyfriend, Parker. I noticed right off that there was something different about him, but couldn't quite figure out what it was.

"Hi, Parker," I said, refusing to feel foolish for having been caught playing with Reggie.

"Hey, Kate," he answered. "Is Josie home?"

"I wasn't up to the house," I told him. "I was just out taking a walk."

"She ain't home," Reggie said. "She went up to see that guy in the jail."

"What for?" Parker asked, echoing the question in my mind.

"I dunno." Reggie shrugged, gave me a high five, and said, "I gotta get home for lunch."

We watched him amble off, kicking stones in front of him as he went.

Parker looked miserable, let me tell you. The change in him had disappeared, and it was then that I realized what it had been. He'd had a look of confidence about him earlier, something I'd never seen in him before. It was more than gone now.

"What do you think Josie wanted to go see that guy for?" he asked me. He had a pathetic, troubled look on his face.

"Beats me," I shrugged, hoping I didn't look as worried as he did. I sure felt pretty awful.

"I was gonna ask her if she'd like to go for a soda."

"Well, you can go later, I imagine," I said.

"Yeah, I guess so." He left then, walking with his shoulders slumped.

All the way home I told myself I wasn't going to go to see Randy until after supper. I decided to pick out some books to take so they'd be ready when I went. I chose *The Catcher in the Rye*, *Seventeen*, and *To Kill a Mockingbird*.

I carried them downstairs to put on the hall table but instead walked out the front door and found myself almost running toward the jail. A great feeling of panic had taken over, and there was just no way I could keep myself from going right then and there.

I was out of breath when I got to the top of the stairs. Officer Johnson was on duty, sitting with his chin resting on his hand. He looked frumpled and tired. I wondered if he and his new wife had been up late fighting. He sure didn't look happy, like he had the first month he'd been married.

"Afternoon, Officer," I said politely.

He nodded without answering, and when I told him I'd brought some books up for Randy he just waved me toward the back room.

I heard Josie's voice before I got to the turn in the hall. It was in what I thought of as high performance mode, full of flirtation and running over with honey.

"Oh, Randy, you're so funny," she was saying. I could picture her standing there with her big eyes shining and her red lips in that smile that just won the boys over like crazy.

I stopped dead in my tracks, feeling a sick rage build up in me. So that was her game. She knew I liked Randy and was getting even with me for our fight by coming here to flirt with him.

"I sure am glad you came up today, Josie," I heard Randy say.

As quietly as possible I went back to the main room and asked Officer Johnson if I could just leave the books with him instead because I was in a hurry. He pointed to a bare spot on the desk with a grunt. I sat the books there before hurrying down the stairs and outside.

I really needed fresh air at that moment. I felt like I could hardly breathe. Something squeezed and ached in my chest. I knew I was about to cry any minute and didn't want to disgrace myself on the street so I ran through the path at the back of Mr. Flaherty's yard and went off into the woods.

The path in the woods was overgrown to some extent, and branches got in my way as I wandered along. My sight was kind of blurred and every so often I'd miss a branch, discovering it when it slapped against me. At last, feeling I was far enough back that no one could hear me, I sat down on a fallen tree and sobbed.

Not more than five minutes could have passed when I became aware of the sound of feet coming along the path. I wiped my eyes and nose quick on the back of my arm.

"Kate?" Mark came into view. "Kate, are you all right?"

"Now what brought you here?" I asked, surprised and glad it was him and no one else. There are times when a little brother is truly the only person in the whole world you want around.

"I was coming out of the five-and-dime and I saw you run through Mr. Flaherty's yard, so I followed you. You looked upset." He sat down beside me on the tree.

"I'm glad you came," I told him. I didn't want him worrying that he wasn't welcome.

He reached a hand over and took one of mine and held it.

"I don't like it when you're sad, Kate," he said simply.

"I don't like it much myself," I admitted with a rueful laugh. "I'll tell you, Mark, growing up is real hard sometimes. All kinds of feelings get in you and a person hardly knows what to do with them."

"What kind of feelings?"

The words were right in my mouth to tell him that he was too young to understand, but I remembered how I hated it when Momma told me that when I was younger.

"It's just hard to explain, Mark. Half the time I don't even know what I'm feeling myself, or *why*. That's what makes it so difficult. At other times I get to wondering if I might be a bit crazy, because I feel one thing one minute, and it might seem powerful and true, but then just like that," I snapped my fingers, "it can change and be totally different. It's hard to sort it all out, believe me."

"Is it because you're dying?" he asked. His face looked frightened. I think he was wanting to be helpful and if it was about that there'd be nothing he could do.

"I guess that's part of it," I said. "I guess it's because all the things that happen to a teenager are happening to me, getting me ready for being grown up, but it's not exciting the way it should be because I know I'm not *going* to grow up. It's like getting ready to go on a long journey and then finding out you're really on a dead-end road."

I looked down and saw that he was crying. For a second or two I felt guilty for making him sad, but it's not my fault things are the way they are. And I thought it might be what he needed, to cry and let himself feel what he was feeling.

For a moment it was like Mark wasn't my brother, but just a little boy who has to get ready to lose his sister. It was kind of weird to see him in that light. I'd always looked at him in relation to me, and not so much as a person all by himself.

So I held him nestled against me and didn't tell him that everything was going to be all right.

CHAPTER TEN

I didn't go back up to the jail that evening, nor the next day. Mostly I just moped around the house feeling horrible.

Around the middle of the afternoon on Friday Josie phoned. If anyone else had answered I'd have told them I didn't feel like talking, but as luck had it I answered it myself.

"Hi, Kate?" she said, sounding every bit as guilty as I knew her to be. "How's it going?"

"Fine," I said shortly.

"I was just going to get an ice cream and I thought maybe you'd like to come along," she said. "My treat."

As if I was going to let her soothe her feelings of guilt with an ice cream!

"No, thank you," I answered, being careful not to offer an excuse or explanation for not going.

There was a moment of silence before she said, "Uh, okay then. Some other time," and hung up. I felt a tiny bit of satisfaction to hear the misery in her voice, although it wasn't nearly what she deserved to suffer.

Just think of it! My best friend for all these years, turning on me and betraying me over a silly argument. Every time I thought of her sitting there smiling at Randy, flirting with him too, when she knew he was special to me, why it was enough to make my blood boil.

"Who was that, Kate?" Momma asked from the other room. I felt annoyed to have to answer.

"It was for me."

"Well, who was it?" she pressed.

"Josie."

"What did she want?"

"Nothing, really," I said.

Parents do that to their children all the time. Have you ever noticed? And can you just imagine how they'd react if we did the same thing to them? If I were to start asking Momma who was on the phone and what did they want about one of her calls, she'd put me in my place but quick!

I wasn't really mad at Momma though. It was like there was this anger in me that was looking for someone to chase and it didn't much care who or why. I decided I'd best be by myself for a bit.

I went outside and wandered into the backyard. Momma's flower garden ran along the fence, bordered in by round rocks she'd painted white. It was a pretty amazing sight, colours waving and shimmering.

I lay down under the oak tree, glad that the grass needed cutting, and watched the leaves rustle above me. In few months acorns would start falling, green little faces with funny brown hats.

Two years ago Mark and I had gathered what seemed to be thousands of them and put them in a box in the basement for the winter. Come spring, we'd soaked some in water until a few swelled up and split. We planted those and two of them grew, little red tongues rising up out of the ground, stretching up into frail little saplings and sporting perfect tiny oak leaves.

It was the most amazing thing, how rainstorms could come with high winds that would almost knock a grown man over, and those tiny oak trees just stood their ground, clutching their leaves and refusing to be beaten. They were a good foot and a half high this year.

I must have fallen asleep out there, but just barely. You know how it is when you can wake up and sort of feel that you've been absent for a few minutes, but you know you're not rested enough to have slept longer than that. The sun was warm on me and I willed myself to drift off again, but then I became aware of a tickle on me.

I looked down and there was a honeybee crawling along my arm. I had a great-uncle who died from a bee sting. He was allergic, and the story went that when he got stung he puffed up like a lumpy red balloon and couldn't breathe. It was strange to think of something as small as a bee being able to kill a person.

I watched the bee then, making like it was his perfect right to wander up and down my arm. I wasn't afraid of it or anything. Momma had taught me and Mark that if you don't bother them they'll just fly away and not sting you. I knew that was right, 'cause I'd done just that lots of times and hadn't been stung.

But today, for some reason, I reached my hand over and brushed the bee and he parked his rear end good and close to my skin and sank his stinger into my arm. Then he flew away. I wondered if he was pleased that he'd taught me a lesson, but that was a foolish thought. Bees don't have emotions. Do they?

The spot where he'd stung got a red lump on it. It didn't hurt too much, though. I realized suddenly that I was disappointed about that.

I had this strange wish that more bees, lots more, would come and sting me until my whole body was aching.

And then I was crying, sobbing and gulping air, and it wasn't because of the bee sting, or because I was dying. I just cried and cried and had no idea why.

After a while I got a thought in my head that I was crying about Randy, but that didn't make too much sense. His situation was bad and all, but not like mine. It was a weird feeling, and I had nothing to compare it with.

It was like a queer ache that started in the middle of me and filled me up. You know what it's like when you toss a big stone into a clear pond and there's a splash and after that ripples from where it landed spread out and out and out? Like that. I could tell where it began, but it didn't exactly end anywhere.

A thought struck me. It was that I should never have asked to go up to the jail in the first place. If I hadn't, I wouldn't be feeling like this. But as soon as that thought came it got chased out because the idea of never having met Randy was worse than what I was feeling, worse than anything.

I looked down at the red lump on my arm and wondered if the ache inside me was evident in any way. I sure didn't want it to be. What if people could look at me and tell that I had this strange sadness in me? It worried me, the notion of being discovered, although I didn't know for *what*.

I got up and snuck into the house through the basement entry to avoid Momma's prying eye. Momma can pretty much tell when something is wrong with anyone at all.

It was dark down there. I've never liked the dark. When I was smaller, I was terrified to get out of bed when the room was dark. I was sure that someone was under the bed and was going to grab my ankle the second it hit the floor. I would stand up on the bed and jump over as far as possible and then run to the doorway and snap on the light. Funny thing was, as soon as the light was on, I knew there was no one under the bed at all, and never once kneeled down to look like I'd meant to when it was dark.

Now I can get out of bed without all that rigmarole, but I still get a tiny wash of relief after my foot's been on the floor for a few seconds and nothing has grabbed my ankle. And I still get that light turned on pretty darn fast.

Anyway, wander, wander. How anyone could ever get through all these sidetracks I take I can't picture, but then no one is ever likely to read any of this so I guess it doesn't much matter.

So there I was downstairs in the dark, and I confess the basement isn't my favourite place anyway. The light switch is at the top of the stairs going into the hallway. Daddy always says he's going to add another switch to the outside entrance, which got added after the house was built, but so far he never has.

I took a deep breath, and I think I was unconsciously holding it as I started up the stairs, but I'm not sure about that. I was on the third step from the bottom, not losing any time in heading up, when something brushed against my leg and made a noise. It startled me so that I screamed and jumped back. I grabbed for the railing, but missed it and landed on the cement floor, where I lay more dazed than hurt.

The door upstairs opened and Momma turned on the light and hurried down to me.

"Land sakes, Kate!" she cried. "What on earth happened?"

As soon as the light went on Sammy went tearing up the stairs and disappeared down the hall. I explained to Momma how he'd been on the step and I hadn't known 'cause I couldn't see him and he'd scared me and I'd fallen.

"But what were you doing down here in the first place?" she asked.

"I live here, remember?" I said, hoping that flippancy would ward off any further questions. It didn't work, of course. Mothers aren't that easily put off.

"Yes, but what were you doing in the basement?" she pressed.

"Nothing, really," I said. "I just came in this way. I was outside and it was warm in the yard and I thought I'd cool off by coming in through the basement."

She didn't look exactly convinced, but she didn't ask any more questions and instead helped me to my feet, holding my arm all the way up the stairs.

I noticed for the rest of the day that Momma kept looking at me funny, like she was trying to figure something out and just couldn't. That was a relief to me. I decided that if Momma couldn't tell I had this ache in me, and why, then it was unlikely that anyone could.

CHAPTER ELEVEN

I woke up during the night with the realization that someone was walking around downstairs. I've noticed that since I got sick I wake up really easy whereas I used to sleep like a log. I guess in a way I'm awake all the time in terms of awareness, with this thing going on inside me and quietly taking away my life. Since I have no control over that, I think I just want to feel in control of other things. Noticing things, hearing them and seeing them in a new light, have all been part of, well, part of dying.

I guess it makes sense that I have a far greater appreciation of what living means. And also more of an understanding that there are limits in everything, and that the greatest limit is time.

Anyway, as I started to say before I got sidetracked (again!) I heard someone downstairs. I slid out of bed, half fuzzy with sleep but curious too, and crept down the hall, taking care not to step on the spot on the floor that creaks. I got halfway down the stairs when I saw that there was a light on in the kitchen.

Can't be a burglar, I thought, they don't turn lights on. That was the first that I realized I'd thought it might be a burglar. I peered over the railing and saw Daddy's shape outlined in the kitchen doorway at the end of the hall. His arm was bent like he had something in his hand and his head was tilted to one side studying whatever it was.

I tiptoed down the rest of the stairs, though it crossed my mind that he might not want to be disturbed, and went down the hall.

"Daddy?" I said quietly.

He started anyway, turning to face me. I guess if you think you're alone, it doesn't matter how soft a person speaks to you, you'd still be surprised to hear a voice.

I got closer to him; my eyes were adjusting to the light in the background and I saw that he was crying. I stood there, not sure of what to say or do.

"Why?" he asked. It hung there between us, me not knowing exactly what he was asking, and him sort of looking through me as though someone behind me might step up and answer his question at any minute.

He stepped forward and put his arms around me. I saw that in his right hand he held my school picture from last year. His shoulders were shaking and in a minute I noticed that I was crying too. I wasn't crying for me either. And it wasn't exactly for him, so much as just because he was crying.

"It seems that I have peace," he said. "I think I have it and then it flies away as though it's never been there at all. Then anger comes and I know it's wrong. I try to trust. I really try to have faith. But there's got to be a reason and there just can't be any reason and none of it makes sense."

I wanted to comfort him. But I thought if God couldn't comfort him, what could I do? Or maybe God sent me down there to do something, but nothing rose up in my mind as being the right thing to say, so I just kept on standing there and saying nothing. I remember wishing I wasn't dying so this moment wouldn't be happening, because it was just so sad, and it was awkward and horrible.

I guess that's what death is to the living. I wonder what death is for the dead.

It's weird because this is happening to me, and yet even though I know I'm going to die, I'm still alive. It's real, and yet it almost isn't, and there are many, many questions in my mind that can't be answered. That must have been how Daddy felt.

The only other time in my life that I saw Daddy cry was when Grandpa passed away. I was twelve then. Mark and I were doing our homework at the kitchen table when someone came to the door. Momma called Daddy and he went to talk to the gentleman there. They talked really quiet so Mark and I couldn't hear anything much, but I remember Daddy thanking the man for coming.

After that he came into the kitchen and told us that Grandpa had died. His mouth was twisted and then tears came and he looked smaller than I'd ever seen him look before.

I'd gone and hugged Daddy and cried with him, but it was different from what was going on now. At that time, I'd been much more outside his grief.

Later on I got thinking about how each relationship in a family is joined and yet has private factors. And grief is one of the most private things there can be. No matter how bad I felt for Daddy when Grandpa died, I couldn't feel what he felt. I could only feel my own sadness.

I wonder how it will be for Momma and Daddy and Mark when I die. I think they'll be alone, each of them, in a large sense, even though they'll try to comfort each other. It's strange to consider how much, and in what ways, a single person's death affects others.

Half lost in my thoughts, I noticed after a few moments that Daddy was talking again.

"Remember when we spent the summer on the lake, at the cottage?"

It had been a good summer in lots of ways. Daddy had taken a whole month off, two weeks in July and two in August, and the rest of the time Momma, Mark, and I had stayed there and he'd just come on weekends. Mark and I had spent a lot of time together, swimming, walking on the shore, exploring in the woods, and going out in the boat, although Momma gave us such a long lecture on boat safety every time we went that it was almost not worth the bother.

"I remember."

"You were so happy." He looked down at the floor. "How can things have changed so much?"

"But I'm not unhappy now, Daddy," I said. "In a way, I'm happier, because I'm aware of good things more than I ever was before. And I appreciate everything more." I had a hard time explaining that to him, but in the end I think he felt soothed, so maybe God did send me to talk to him after all.

I went back to my room after and got out my copy of *Oliver Twist*. I held it open and let the note Randy had written to me fall on the bed. I read it over again, as if I didn't know it by heart already, and then put it away and crawled into bed.

For a long time I looked out the window, watching the stars flicker against the black sky. Just as I was falling off to sleep, I wondered if maybe Randy was awake and looking at the same stars.

The thought made me sad and happy all at once.

CHAPTER TWELVE

I slept in the next morning, which I almost never do, since I hate to find the day half gone when I get up. When I wandered downstairs I found the house empty, although I could hear Momma in the backyard working on her garden.

She used to sing a lot of weird old songs when she was gardening, and Mark and I would sometimes hide around the corner and giggle at them. It started to get alarming, though, when I realized that I knew a lot of the words to some of them. I mean, how horrible would it be if I was somewhere with friends and all of a sudden I found myself singing one of them, without realizing I'd been doing it?

I could just imagine their reaction if I burst into some old people's song and had to be reminded that it's 1962 and maybe I should get with the modern times.

Heaven knows what kind of razzing, or, even worse, nickname, I'd get out of it. I didn't care to risk that.

Lately, though, Momma tends to sing hymns, when she sings at all, which isn't nearly as often as she used to. Today she was just humming and sure enough it was a hymn.

I opened the fridge when I got to the kitchen, although I wasn't particularly hungry. It's kind of a rule in our house that you have to eat something for breakfast. If I've heard Momma say that breakfast is the most important meal of the day once, I've heard it a million times.

There was nothing in the fridge that appealed to me, so I turned to see if there were any bananas on the counter. That's when I noticed the envelope on the table. It was addressed to me.

I picked it up with my heart pounding all of a sudden. Maybe Randy had written to say that he missed me and wanted me to come and see him again.

Forgetting about the most important meal of the day, I hurried back to my room and closed the door. I sat on the edge of my bed with the envelope in my hand, and just looked at it for a few moments. For some reason, I was almost scared to open it.

The address on the outside was printed, so I couldn't compare it to Randy's handwriting from his letter. There was no return address or anything, but it was a local postmark, and it had been mailed the day before.

Finally, with my fingers all trembling, I opened it and drew out a single sheet of paper and read, neatly printed in the centre of the page:

Mrs. Maryanne Richards
is most honoured by
Miss Kate Benchworth's
request.

Down in the right-hand corner were the words "4:00 a.m. at the playground."

My disappointment that the letter wasn't from Randy disappeared quickly. I'd almost forgotten about my note to Maryanne. I guess I hadn't really expected an answer at all. But here it was, and as clear as could be she was saying I could join her on her walk.

Then I got wondering what day she meant. All it said was four in the morning. What if she'd meant today, and I'd missed the chance. But no, she'd realize that it would take a day for her letter to reach me. She must mean tomorrow morning.

I knew right away that this was to be a secret, which led to the next worry. Momma must have been the one to put the letter on the table and was certain to ask me about it. I heard the door open only moments later, and her footsteps go into the kitchen.

Sure enough, as soon as I'd gone back downstairs, she turned from the stove with the question on her face before the words even came out of her mouth. Have you ever noticed how you can tell just from their eyes that someone is going to ask you something? Well, Momma's eyes had that "here comes a question" look.

"I see that you had mail, Kate," she said. Then she waited, and I knew she was expecting me to tell her all about it without making her actually ask.

"Yes." I was lost for anything else to add. It looked like I was hiding something, which I guess in a way I was.

She didn't wait long. That's one thing about Momma. She doesn't keep you in the dark when she wants to know something. I have some friends who complain that their mothers are sneaky, and try to find things out by tricking them, or even worse, snooping behind their back. Not Momma. She does all her prying above board.

"Who was it from?" she asked, right out.

"It's kind of private, Momma," I answered. I was pretty sure that would never satisfy her and more questions would have to be fended off. But she surprised me, as she sometimes does.

"Oh," with just a short pause, and, "all right then," was all she said, and then she went on to talk about something else and never mentioned it again.

Of course there was still the matter of getting out of the house undetected in the morning, and the question of how to explain my absence in the event that I was missed. I decided to worry about both of those things when the time came. As long as no one happened to hear my alarm ring, I might be able to pull it off without anyone being the wiser.

I thought about Maryanne most of the rest of that day, which was good since it took my mind off Randy, not to mention Josie's betrayal.

The last time I'd seen Maryanne Richards was about two years after her husband left her and it was probably close to the last appearance she made in public. She'd been seen in town so rarely after Jeff walked out on her that people tended to look at her and whisper on the few occasions that she showed up somewhere. Finally, she stopped going anywhere altogether, and no one had seen her for close to three years.

I'd been in the drugstore, getting a piece of bristol board for a school project. As usual, I'd waited until the last minute to do the assignment, although I'd had nearly three weeks to get it done. I always seemed to be enthusiastic when we had a project to do, and would come up with all kinds of great ideas of what I could do, and the next thing I knew I only had a couple of days left until it was due, and I had to rush and do something easy.

Anyway, there I was, standing in the aisle where the school supplies were, when Maryanne came into the store. I had a clear view of her from where I was standing, and I confess I couldn't help staring at her. She put me in mind right away of a big walking dough woman. It wasn't even so much her size, which was enormous, but her pasty white face with dark little eyes squinting out like raisins.

Everyone around kind of stopped what they were doing, looked right at her, and then lowered their heads as if they'd found the most interesting thing in the world to look at on the floor.

She waddled up to the counter with her purchases and the salesgirl's voice was a little too high and cheerful, almost to the point of being brittle, as she spoke to her.

"Afternoon, Mrs. Richards. How are you today?" the girl queried.

"Fine," was the single-word answer. It was said in a way that told the counter girl and everyone else in hearing that there wasn't going to be any further conversation.

I remember how that word echoed over and over in my head for a long time afterward. It was about the saddest sound I'd ever heard. In one syllable, she had managed to put up some sort of shield to defend herself from unwelcome chatter. At the same time, there was a lonesomeness in it, like she was putting people off because she had to, like she had no choice.

Maryanne had faded into the background of local gossip after a while. But every so often someone would mention her name and there'd be the usual comments about how sad it was that her husband had left her or how tragic that she had become a recluse, but inevitably the comments ended up centred on her corpulence. There was always a distasteful tone carrying judgement and a degree of smugness when her size was discussed.

Even at the time, I understood that the world viewed obesity as a sin and the other things were seen almost as a punishment that she deserved because of it. The undercurrent of this ran in every other thing said about Maryanne. Why would her husband want to remain married to a woman who embarrassed him? Or why should she expect to have friends?

Now, I'm not claiming to be wiser or better than anyone else, but it seems to me that a person's worth should be based on who they are, and not what they look like. Maybe I feel that way because here I am, fourteen and skinny with short tufts of hair that I can't do much with no matter how hard I try. I'd hate for anyone to just see the outside and decide what kind of person I am by looking at me. You should get to know people and make up your mind if you like them because of their personality, not their appearance. That's what I think, anyway.

In any case, the more time that passed, the greater the mystery that grew around her. I doubt that she would have welcomed the curiosity, or the kitchen discussions, but people had developed a hankering to know what made her choose a life of total solitude.

And now, here I was, about to go walking with the town enigma.

Chapter Thirteen

As it turned out, I needn't have worried about my alarm waking anyone in the morning. I must have been too excited to sleep, because I woke up before it had a chance to ring. I've noticed though, that lots of times when I set my alarm for something important, I wake up first, like there's a clock inside that sends me a signal to get up.

I slipped out of bed and went to the bathroom downstairs to get washed up and dressed, seeing as how the old pipes in the upstairs bathroom sometimes make this eerie sound like something is in the pipe crying. I was careful to walk close to the wall going down the stairs 'cause the creaks in the steps are right in the middle.

I had put a note on my bed just in case someone went into my room and discovered I wasn't there. It probably wouldn't keep me from getting in trouble, but at least no one would have to worry. The note just said: "Couldn't sleep. Gone for short walk. Back soon."

Out the back door, through our yard and then the neighbour's before I hit the street, I figured I was home free. It was about a ten-minute walk to the playground, which is on the elementary school grounds.

I remember how nervous I was on my first day of school, going there. Momma took me and we went into a big room, which I later learned was the auditorium. There were tables set up and Momma led me to one that had "ABC" on it. I was kind of insulted, 'cause I already knew my ABCs and I thought she was signing me up to learn them or something.

She explained, in answer to my protests, that it was the table for everyone whose last names started with one of those letters. From there, she took me to a classroom and introduced me to my teacher, Mr. Carmichael. It was his first year teaching and he was friendly and patient for about two weeks. After that it seemed we were always giving him a headache with our noise. I worried a lot about Mr. Carmichael and his headaches. I thought for sure he'd never make it to the end of the school year without us killing him, as he often assured us we were trying to do. I didn't want to be responsible for Mr. Carmichael dying and tried to be quiet, but it was so easy to forget.

I got thinking about poor Mr. Carmichael on the way to meet Maryanne and wondered how he'd managed to put up with the noise in his own house after he got married. He and his wife had five children, one right after the other, so I doubt it was too peaceful at their place. I'd seen Mrs. Carmichael around town with the children and she seemed really calm. The kids would be jumping and running around, whooping and hollering, and she'd never even seem to notice. Maybe Mr. Carmichael's headaches got better. I hope so.

The playground is pretty big and I wasn't sure where to wait for Maryanne, so I wandered over to the swings, which are in the middle, and sat on one of them, watching for her.

She came along only a few minutes later and startled me with a soft, "Good morning, Kate."

I near fell off the swing right then and there. It was Maryanne all right, or what was left of her anyway, but if I'd met her on the street I'd have walked right on by and never known who she was. She must have lost a hundred and fifty pounds at least. There I'd been, waiting for an enormous woman, and here she was, just an average size.

I noticed after a few seconds that she was smiling, and it became equally obvious why. There I was with my mouth hanging open and my eyes near falling out of their sockets. On top of that I realized I hadn't even answered her greeting. I gathered the few wits I had left about me and managed to say hello back.

"I guess you were expecting someone a little bigger," she said, her smile growing. "Or, I should say, a lot bigger."

There seemed no polite way to answer that. I didn't like to admit that she was right, but the truth of what she'd said was undeniable. Finally I ventured a smile back and made some remark about not having seen her for a long time.

"No, I've not been a very public person for a long while," she answered. "I guess you could say that I've been hiding."

"But why?" I had to ask.

"I think that, like most of the town, you probably know part of the answer to that," she said softly. "Come, let's walk and I'll tell you the rest of it."

So we ventured off, heading toward the outskirts of town. I was curious, but figured that Maryanne would talk when she was ready, so for the first while we just went along in silence.

"It's fitting that I'm going to tell this to you, Kate," she began when our pace had steadied to an easy stride. "I was surprised and very pleased to get your note the other day. I'd been wondering how to start, and with whom. You were the right person, and I saw this opportunity as part of fate."

I'm sure she saw the astonishment in my face at that remark, but she continued without remarking on it.

"When Jeff moved out of the house, out of town for that matter, I was embarrassed. I knew that people had always assumed he'd married me because he thought he'd be given my father's business someday. The funny thing was, I wondered it myself, but didn't let it stand in the way of marrying him. I wanted to have a husband and children and a home of my own. I thought if I was a good wife, he'd love me someday, even if he hadn't when he married me."

"Did you love him?" I interrupted.

She paused at the question, as though considering it for the first time. "I don't really know," she said finally. "At the time I thought that I did, but looking back I couldn't say for sure. We hadn't dated very long when he proposed, and I was excited and happy to think that someone wanted to marry me. I hadn't had any other boyfriends before Jeff."

A thought darted through my mind that I hadn't had any boyfriends before Randy. I pushed it away, feeling foolish and wondering where it had come from.

"Were you happy together?"

"Oh," she smiled an odd, sad smile, "at first I was very happy. I had a husband, sort of a trophy. But it didn't last very long." A long pause. "I could see that Jeff wasn't happy. He was kind enough at the beginning, but something was missing. I knew then that he didn't love me, couldn't love me. I started to feel afraid all the time."

"Afraid?"

"Afraid that he would leave me. That everyone would know and I'd look foolish. It was horrible then, always trying too hard, on the verge of panic, wanting to make him love me and knowing I couldn't."

I reached out, without thinking about it, and touched Maryanne's arm.

"No, Kate," she drew in a long breath, "don't feel sorry for me. It's the worst thing a person can do. Things are just the way they are. I spent years feeling sorry for myself, hiding, ashamed. What a waste."

We turned then, along the old bike path leading through the woods and down to the river. A squirrel jabbered angrily as we passed its territory.

"Well," Maryanne continued after a few moments, "I might have spent the rest of my life in the house, hiding, except for you."

"Except for *me*?"

"Yes. I hear things, especially in the summer when the windows are open. Neighbours talking in their houses, people on the street. I hear a lot. And I heard about you. Your illness. I barely knew who you were, because, of course, anyone wrapped up in self-pity doesn't pay a lot of attention to others. But I heard and I started thinking."

A sudden wave of nausea hit me and I stopped walking. Maryanne turned and looked at me, her face full of concern.

"Why, Kate!" she cried. "You're as white as a sheet. Do you need to rest?"

I couldn't answer her because I was trying to fight down the urge to throw up. It wasn't the first time I'd felt that way in the morning, but usually I could lie down and it would pass. This time I could see it wasn't going to go away. I stumbled off the path, leaned over, and began retching.

I felt Maryanne's hand on my back, touching me lightly. I wished that she wasn't there, even though she was trying to help. It's not a time when you want anyone watching. Afterward, I felt weak and I was pretty sure I was going to cry. I didn't want her to see that either, but it just kept on getting bigger and bigger, the need to cry, and finally I did.

I realized after a moment that Maryanne was crying too. She put her arm around me and we just stood there for a while, until I was all cried out.

"Dear, little one," she said softly. She took the water bottle she wore in a long pouch around her neck and gave me a drink. The water was cool and soothing but I could only take a few sips.

"I'm all right now," I said, gathering myself together. It's amazing how you can force yourself to feel better even when all you want to do is lie down and rest. I was exhausted but still very curious to hear the rest of Maryanne's story.

She insisted that we turn back toward town, although it was only a few more minutes' walk to the river. So we headed along, and I got to feeling a lot better, and after a little while we resumed our conversation.

"I began thinking about you a lot, which was a big change for me." I must have looked puzzled again, because she continued by saying, "When you spend all of your time alone feeling sorry for yourself, it's not all that common to spend much time thinking about someone else. In your case, I found that I was. And the more I thought about you, and your illness, the more I realized that I was committing a horrible wrong."

We paused, and Maryanne gave me another drink from her water bottle. "It was a cathartic moment for me, the day that I saw my life for what it was. There I was, hiding from the world, but more than that, hiding from myself. Instead of making the best of my life and myself, I spent all my time wrapped tight in self-pity. I comforted myself with food, which only made things worse. I was ashamed to be seen in public because I could just imagine people whispering behind my back, saying things like, 'No wonder her husband left her, look at how fat she is.'"

I knew she was telling the truth because of all the conversations I'd heard over the years.

"And here you were, a lovely little girl with such a heavy burden to carry. I heard about your illness, and then I heard people talking about how bravely you were facing it, how you refused to give in and feel sorry for yourself. Well, Kate, let me tell you, that woke me up like nothing ever had before. I had a choice too, I'd had one all along. I could have been brave and faced my problems and overcome them, but I hadn't. That was when I decided I was going to change all of that. I was going to be brave, just as you were brave."

"But, you still don't go places," I pointed out.

"No, not yet. But I will soon. The first thing I had to do was overcome some of the reasons I couldn't face people. Like my weight. I began eating sensibly, and walking early every morning when no one was around. Now, I'm almost ready to face the world again, and to face my own life."

"Maryanne," I said impulsively, "would you come to dinner at our house one night?"

She paused. I knew it was a big question. I knew it would be hard for her, that very first time she stepped across the invisible line she'd drawn that kept her apart from other people.

"Yes," she spoke at last, "yes I will, Kate." Her words were calm and steady, but I could see the struggle to overcome fear flickering in her eyes.

CHAPTER FOURTEEN

It was still dark outside when I got home again. I slipped back into my room without anyone waking and crawled into bed. For a while I lay there trying to get back to sleep, but there was too much going on in my head. It's nearly impossible to sleep when you've got a whole bunch of thoughts running around and around in your mind.

After an hour or so I heard Momma and Daddy getting up. Momma always gets up with Daddy when he's getting ready for work, and if I'm awake I can hear them talking in low, quiet murmurs. It's a nice sound, soft and kind. Some of my friends have commented to me about the way my parents talk to each other, never cross or rude.

Josie's parents often raise their voices to each other and sometimes say mean things. I would probably fall over in a dead faint if I heard my folks talk the way the Spencers do. They argue sometimes, but they don't put each other down or yell over disagreements.

I waited for a little while and then got up and went downstairs to join them. I'd decided I was going to have to tell them about my walk with Maryanne or I'd never be able to explain why I wanted Momma to invite her to dinner.

"Why, Kate, you're up awfully early today."

"I've been up for a while, Momma," I answered, then plunged in and told her and Daddy about my note to Maryanne and her answer and our walk that morning. I left out most of the things we'd talked about because I didn't want to betray Maryanne's privacy or her trust in telling me things about her life and feelings.

"Maryanne Richards?" Momma repeated several times, as though it was just too much to believe.

"I asked her if she'd come here for dinner some evening," I added after I'd finished telling my story. "I hope that was okay."

"Why, of course it's okay, dear." I knew Momma would never refuse to do anything kind for anyone, so her answer was pretty much expected.

Not one word was said about me hiding my plans or sneaking out of the house at that hour of the morning. I'd been all ready for a big lecture, but then, you never really know with parents. At times it seems you'll be in trouble for sure, and they just let it go.

When Daddy was leaving for work, he even stopped and turned to me and said, "You're a good girl, Kate." I wasn't sure if he meant I was good for telling them what I'd done, or for doing it in the first place. Daddy doesn't express himself very clearly when he's saying something like that and I'm often left to figure it out for myself.

Momma and I ate breakfast together after Daddy was gone and I could tell she would have liked to find out more about Maryanne, but she didn't ask any questions. She told me that I could invite Maryanne over any time I liked.

"Just let me know the day before so I can plan a nice dinner."

And that was it. I gave her a huge hug when the dishes were washed and we left the kitchen, Momma to start some laundry, and me to write down some more of this story.

At around ten-thirty Momma called me downstairs. When I got to the bottom of the stairs I could see Josie standing in the doorway. Her face was sad and determined-looking all at once, and I knew it wasn't going to be easy to put her off this time.

To tell the truth, I guess I wasn't all that keen on putting her off. It seemed that my anger had burned out and I was left feeling almost silly about the whole thing. I'm not sure how it had changed, because I'd been certain that I'd be mad at Josie forever, and yet I wasn't. I was actually kind of glad to see her.

"Kate," she started, and then trailed off. It struck me that she'd rehearsed what she was going to say and then couldn't remember it. Or maybe was afraid it would come out all wrong, like when you practise saying something and get all mixed up and end up blurting out parts of it that don't quite connect.

"Hi, Josie." I smiled when I spoke, but it came out feeling like the kind of smile you make when you're posing for a picture and feel kind of awkward.

Even so, her face lit right up and she just rushed over and started babbling a lot of confused stuff about being sorry and having her feelings hurt and how I meant more than some old boy, and a bunch of other things. There was no mention of how she'd gone to flirt with Randy, knowing full well how much I liked him. Then I realized that she didn't know I had seen her there.

"Let's just forget the whole thing," I said when she paused to draw a breath. She nodded happily and then suggested right away that we think of something to do for the rest of the day.

We headed out of the house a few moments later without any clear idea of where we were going. Josie was talking non-stop but not really saying anything. She does that when she's nervous, just chatters on and on, and I've learned it's best to just let her go. There's no point in trying to have an actual conversation with her until she's calmed down, and anyway, the babbling seems to help her get rid of the nervousness.

Then she mentioned Randy and I started to pay attention.

"And he asked me yesterday how come you never go to see him anymore."

"Oh, you saw Randy yesterday?" I asked, with my chest tightening.

"I've seen him pretty much every day since I first met him," she answered with such innocence in her voice that I hardly knew how to respond. "It must be pretty awful for him to be stuck in that little cell all by himself, so I try to take a few minutes to drop in and visit when I can."

I was curious to know how he was, but reluctant to ask. Josie had taken over what I viewed as my role in visiting Randy, and it seemed I was going to have to accept that and forget about any crazy ideas I might have had that he and I were friends in a special way.

"So, what do you think? Are you going to go up or not?"

I realized that Josie had continued talking about it while I was lost in thought. This forced me to ask her what she meant.

"To visit Randy!" There was exasperation in her voice. Josie is not the most patient person in the whole world, and doesn't like having to repeat herself. This has always been a problem in our friendship, since my mind often wanders off right in the middle of conversations.

"I don't see why he'd want me to go visit him again," I said a little coldly. "After all, he has you going there every day."

Josie stopped walking and wheeled around to face me. It was such a sudden movement that I almost lost my balance in stopping to look back at her.

"So, that's what this whole fight has really been about!" Her face grew pink. "You think I've been up there butting in on your boyfriend."

"He's not my boyfriend," I retorted hotly.

"Well, you sure wouldn't know that to hear him talk," she answered. "It's 'Kate said this' and 'Kate said that' and 'I wish Kate would come up again' every time I talk to him."

I was as close to being speechless as I've ever been when I heard these words. Randy, talking about me! Randy wanting me to visit him!

"But, what about you?" I asked when I could get my voice to work again.

"Me?" Josie laughed hard, throwing her head back. "As if he'd be interested in me after he's met you."

This was almost too much for me to imagine, and I wondered if she was making a joke at my expense. What boy would prefer me, scrawny and stubby-haired, over a beautiful girl like Josie? It was impossible. Then I was struck with the thought that Josie had told him about my illness. That would explain things. What seemed to be interest was really pity. He was probably feeling sorry for me and was trying to be nice.

"Does Randy know that, I'm, uh, sick?"

"Not that I know of." Josie's answer was quick and guileless enough to convince me that if he knew, she wasn't aware of it. But perhaps someone else had told him. After all, everyone in town knew about it. No doubt someone had mentioned it to him when I was going to see him.

But what if he didn't know? What if he actually liked me, Kate Benchworth?

I had to know. I decided that at the first chance I would go pay him a visit. It would be great to see him again, no matter what.

Josie and I spent the afternoon wandering through town, going from store to store, window-shopping and planning a wardrobe neither one of us could afford. She even tried on a few outfits, and looked spectacular in them. When she tried to persuade me to do the same, I insisted that it was too much bother for something I'd never own anyway. But the truth was I had learned from experience that clothes usually looked a lot better on the mannequins than they did on me. In fact, they often looked better on the hangers! It was a lot more fun to pick out outfits and just *imagine* wearing them.

When it got near dinnertime, I asked Josie if she'd like to come over to eat. To tell the truth, I was glad when she said that she had a date with Parker and had to go home to get ready. We parted for the day with a hug and promise never again to fight over something so silly.

I turned down the street that led to my house with my stomach all queasy and excited. With no plans for the evening, it looked like a good time to see Randy. I hoped we weren't going to eat late!

Chapter Fifteen

My stomach was all in flutters that evening as I dried the dishes Momma sat neatly in the drain tray. I was trying to pay attention to what she was talking about, but my mind was just not on the conversation, and more than once she had to repeat a question. She kept giving me odd looks but didn't come right out and ask me why I was so distracted. I knew she'd like to know, and was surprised yet again that she didn't pry. Momma was turning out to be a pretty neat person.

"Kate?"

I heard my name and drew my attention back from thoughts of Randy and what we'd talk about and whether or not he'd be happy to see me.

"Sorry, Momma. What was that?"

"I just asked if you had any plans this evening." Momma looked slightly exasperated.

My heart kind of slumped at the question, thinking that she was going to ask me to do something. "Uh, I kind of had plans," I mumbled. "Why? Did you want me for anything?"

"No, dear. I was just going to say that if you had something to do I could finish these up myself."

I was awfully tempted to drop the dishtowel and head to the jail, but it seemed wrong, especially since I'd been basically ignoring Momma while we worked. So I told her I was in no hurry and finished the job. It seemed to take forever, since Momma is very particular about making sure every speck is off the plates, and holds the glasses up to the light to check for spots.

Finally, the last pot was dried and put away and I ran up to my room and got a couple of books for Randy. As I headed out the door, Momma called out to me, and I stopped to see what she wanted.

"If you happen to be going to the jail," she said, walking toward me with a brown paper bag in her hand, "please give this to Randy. It's a few of the cookies I baked this afternoon."

I took the bag and noticed that Momma had a long, questioning kind of look in her eyes. It seemed she wanted to say something, like it was right there about to be spoken.

"Did you want anything else, Momma?"

"You like this boy, don't you, Kate?" It was more a statement than a question, and she didn't wait for an answer. "I'd like to have a talk to you, about, well, about boys and things." She must have seen my dismay, because she laughed then. "I don't mean right now, dear. Just sometime soon. Run along now and have a nice visit with your friend."

On the way to the jail I got thinking about the idea of sitting down with Momma and having a talk "about boys and things" and I started giggling and couldn't get stopped. Anyone who saw me must have thought I'd gone completely off the deep end, walking along laughing. I kept picturing Momma trying to talk about boys and sex and stuff, and how hard it would be for her. I bet the entire talk would consist of her trying to say things without actually saying them, and looking at the floor the whole time.

Before I knew it, I was at the jail and running up the stairs. The officer on duty barely glanced up long enough to see me and wave me on through to the back room. Everyone was so nice to Randy now, and even the police working there brought him things to help pass the time. If it had been up to the people of Farrago, they'd have just let him out.

As I got near the end of the hall, I suddenly had a hard time making my legs work. They went all rubbery and weird-feeling, and to make matters worse, my breathing went all funny too. And then there he was, standing up and looking right at me.

"Kate!" His voice sounded happy, which caused my heart to give a little leap. "I heard someone coming and I was hoping it would be you."

"Out of books, are you?" I replied, smiling and hoping all the strange feelings inside me weren't making my face go all twisted or weird looking.

He laughed at that. "Well, I *am* out of books," he admitted, "but I'd be glad to see you anyway. I've been wondering where you were these past few days."

"I have an *awfully* full social calendar," I answered, waving my hand in the air like I'd seen really pretentious characters on TV shows do.

"Oh, do you now?" He laughed again, and I noticed that his eyes lit up when he did. "Well, I'm sure glad you found time in your busy schedule to come and see me."

"Yes, I pencilled you in between my visit with a duchess and a ball I'm to attend later on tonight."

"I'm honoured."

"And so you should be." I reached the books toward him. "I've brought some fine literature so you can improve your mind."

"I hope they improve my mind as much as you improve my moods," he said, taking them. He looked the titles over, smiled, and sat them down on his bed. "Thank you, Kate."

"Josie tells me she's been to see you a few times," I remarked, keeping my voice casual.

"Yes, nice girl." His answer didn't exactly satisfy me. It could have meant almost anything. In spite of the conversation I'd had with her earlier in the day, I was convinced that no boy could actually prefer me over her. Boys just went foolish around Josie.

"She and I have been friends for years and years," I added. "She's very popular."

"I suppose that's partly because she's beautiful."

"She's a good friend, too." I couldn't help the sinking feeling I got from his remark, even though he'd have to be blind not to see how gorgeous Josie was.

"I've appreciated her coming to see me," he added. "The time is long in here, though it's my own fault I'm in this mess."

"Most guys appreciate Josie," I said, trying hard to keep my voice light.

"Probably," he answered, "but I appreciate you the most."

Have you ever had a flash of happiness pass through you so hard and sudden that it left you feeling like your knees might give out? I thought for a second or two that I was going to lose my balance and make a total fool of myself by falling on the floor.

Worse, I could feel my face getting all flushed. And the really weird thing was that all of a sudden I could hardly breathe, much less speak. I must have looked like a real sophisticate standing there all tongue-tied and getting redder with every heartbeat.

Randy seemed to have taken my silence the wrong way, because he started looking as though he regretted saying anything. Maybe he thought I was embarrassed or angry. In any case, he changed the subject before I could regain my voice.

"So, what time is your big ball this evening?" his voice cracked when he spoke, and it sounded so funny that I started laughing.

Of course that made things a whole lot worse and I wished for a moment I hadn't even gone to see him, except for that fact that he'd actually told me he liked me. Well, he hadn't actually said it in those words, but it was pretty clear that's what he meant. And what did I do? Stood there like a perfect dolt without answering, and then laughed like a fool over the squeak in his voice.

I might have had a chance to get the whole misunderstanding straightened out if Randy's mom hadn't chosen that exact moment to come along.

"Why, Kate, dear! How nice to see you." She hurried over and smiled at both Randy and me.

"Good evening, Mrs. Nichols," I stammered, hoping with all my might that the red in my cheeks had faded. "It's nice to see you too, ma'am."

It might have been my imagination, but I'm pretty sure Mrs. Nichols gave me a queer look and I think she knew that something was up all right because she glanced back and forth at Randy and me as if she was trying to figure it out.

Randy started talking to his mom, answering her mother-type questions, and I felt like an eavesdropper who didn't belong there at all. On top of that, Randy was avoiding looking at me. I wanted to fall through a crack in the floor.

As soon as there was a pause in their conversation I grabbed the chance and said I had to get going.

"Oh, don't leave because of me, dear."

"No, ma'am. I just have to get home and get a few things done." It sounded lame even to me.

"Kate has an important ball she has to attend," Randy said, leaning toward his mom and whispering as though sharing a secret.

"Oh, a ball," she smiled and nodded, going along with the joke. "And I suppose there'll be a Prince Charming there, will there?"

"Prince Charmings don't abound in Farrago," I assured her as I began moving toward the hallway.

"Kate?" Randy spoke quickly.

"Yes?"

"Please come up tomorrow." There was disappointment in his face, and I knew he wished I wasn't leaving.

"I mean, if you can."

"I can, and I will," I promised, my spirits lifting. "See you then."

When I got home a short while later I found the house empty. I wandered about for a bit, unable to concentrate enough to read or watch TV or anything. There was a sort of nervous energy in me as I got thinking about Randy and how things had gone. I imagined a lot of conversations between us, with him telling me how much he liked me, and me saying and doing just the right thing. Maybe if I rehearsed scenes in my head, things would go better the next time there was a chance to talk.

I was right in the middle of a fantasy of Randy asking me if I'd be his girlfriend when the phone rudely brought me back to reality.

"Kate?" It was Josie, all breathless. She gets that way when she has interesting news, which usually means gossip of some sort. "Did you hear? Jeff Richards is back in town. Everyone is talking about it."

Well! That *would* be big news in Farrago. I could just imagine the tongues wagging and the speculations flying. Why, if Josie, who hadn't even really known the Richards, was this keen to talk about it, I could only imagine the rest of the town's reaction.

What was Jeff doing here? It had been years since anyone had even heard from him. His own mother told people all the time how heartbroken she was that she hadn't had so much as a letter or phone call since he'd left.

"I blame that woman he married," she would say bitterly. "Jeff would never ignore his own mother if it wasn't for her. She drove him away from all of us."

And now, he was back. I wondered if Maryanne had heard.

CHAPTER SIXTEEN

I just had to talk to her, and so the next morning I got up in time to meet with Maryanne for her morning walk. Since I wasn't sure if she went by the playground where we'd met before, I went straight to her house and waited outside until I saw the side door open.

She didn't seem all that surprised to see me.

"Morning, Kate." Her voice was light and happy. "I thought you might happen along again one of these days. I'm glad to see you."

I found myself staring at her. After all the years of being accustomed to Maryanne being huge and pasty looking, it was still amazing to see her slimmed down and, well, almost pretty. I returned her greeting and we fell into step as though we walked together every day.

"You look nice," I ventured, after a moment. "You really do."

"Thank you, Kate." She seemed a little uncomfortable with the compliment and it occurred to me that she probably hadn't had a whole lot of them in her lifetime.

I remembered the plan to have her as a dinner guest and asked if she would be free to come over the next day. She hesitated slightly, and then agreed after making sure I'd checked it out with Momma.

We walked chatting idly for a few moments, and I was trying to figure out a way to bring up the subject of Jeff, when she sprang it on me.

"I suppose you've heard that my husband is here."

"Yes, I heard that."

"He called yesterday," she paused, and I waited because I could tell she wasn't finished. "He wants to see me."

"Are you going to see him?"

"Yes."

"When?" I knew I shouldn't be asking such personal questions, especially since Maryanne has kept her life private for so long, but it came out before I could stop myself.

"Today. This afternoon."

I managed to get control of my mouth, which you know isn't all that easy for me, and kept from asking her what she thought he wanted.

Turns out, I didn't have to. She seemed anxious to talk about it, and when I thought about the whole thing later, I realized that she really didn't have anyone else to talk to about anything going on in her life.

"I've been wondering, ever since he called, why he's here after all this time. Not a word for years and then the phone rings one day and he's asking to see me."

We turned and entered the playground, where Maryanne stopped and sat on a swing. I plopped down on one beside her and waited for her to go on.

"We're still married, you know." She said this contemplatively. "It may be about that."

"You mean he might want to get back together?"

She laughed at that. "No, I mean he may be here to talk about a divorce. It's so long since he left, and I assume there have been other women. I guess it's likely that he'll want to get married again someday."

That hadn't even occurred to me, and I felt really sad for her. How horrible would it be to have your husband desert you and humiliate you in the whole town's eyes, and then come back some day just to ask for a divorce?

Maryanne didn't seem all that upset, but then, you never know what's going on in someone else. She might be putting on a brave front, and feel just terrible inside.

And here I was, just a kid really, and the only person she had to talk to. I felt pretty useless, and I had no idea what to say, or even if I should say anything at all.

"It will be strange to see him again, after all this time." She rose from the swing and I followed her as she headed across the playground. "I really haven't thought much about Jeff for so long."

"Are you nervous?"

"Yes. I suppose I'm a bit nervous. But not because I think it's going to be traumatic or anything. It stopped hurting long ago. Mostly, I'm just curious about what it will be like to see him."

I was wondering if she'd thought about how amazed her husband would have to be when he saw Maryanne, saw the way she looked now. He couldn't be prepared for the changes in her. Not just physical changes either, she was different altogether.

Almost as though she'd read my mind, she spoke again.

"Jeff doesn't know me anymore. A lot has changed in the past year. The weight and how I feel about myself and life in general. I guess it's going to be quite a shock for him."

The thought made her smile, and that pleased me a whole lot.

"Things are going to change even more for me soon. Now that I'm ready to face the world instead of hiding I'm actually looking forward to life. I was thinking I might like to get a job."

"What kind of job?" I was quite sure Maryanne had never worked and didn't know if she had any kind of training.

"I think I'd like to do interior decorating. I learned a lot when my father had the hardware store, and I've studied some things on my own lately. I think I have a knack for it. You'll have to come and see what I've done with my house. It's not bad."

Another surprising revelation. I'd long had a picture in my mind of Maryanne's house being drab and uncared for. Since she hadn't taken care of herself for so long, it made sense that she wouldn't have bothered much about her surroundings either.

Well! When we finished our walk and got to her house again, she beckoned me to come in. I just stood there in the kitchen in amazement, thinking it was the prettiest room I'd ever seen. That was until we went into the living room. It was breathtaking. The whole house was incredible, rich colours with startling accents.

Maryanne just kept smiling as I repeated "wow" over and over.

"This is unbelievable!" I finally gasped. "You should start your own business."

Have you ever noticed that sometimes you can make a remark like that because it seems really obvious to you, and you can tell by the person's reaction that it had never even occurred to them before? Well, that's the reaction I saw in Maryanne.

Her eyes got a little bigger for a few seconds and then she seemed gone off into her own world. I could almost watch the idea working itself around in her head. It was a few moments before she spoke again, and when she did, all she said was "My own business" in a faraway voice.

I knew the thought was exciting to her, and considering the way I feel when something like that is racing around in my head, I also knew she'd probably like to be alone to think about it some more. So I said goodbye, reminded her about dinner the next evening, and headed off home.

On my way I got thinking more about her meeting with Jeff, and said a silent prayer that it wouldn't be hurtful to Maryanne.

CHAPTER SEVENTEEN

When I got home I was really tired, so I curled up in bed and went back to sleep. When I woke up I discovered that it was after lunch and I was horrified to think of having wasted so much of the day. That was until I got out of bed and found myself running for the bathroom. I didn't quite make it and ended up heaving on the floor in the hallway.

Momma heard the noise and came hurrying to me, leaned down and folded me into her arms, speaking softly, saying it was all right.

It wasn't all right. Not because I made a mess on the floor, but because I knew that I was getting worse. Sometimes I get to wondering exactly how much time I have left, and it causes a sort of panic in me. How many months, weeks, even days do I have left? How many minutes? What will the end be like?

I don't want to die, but I know I'm going to and there's not a thing I can do about it. I guess most people are faced with having to do things they don't want to, but this is a final thing. There's no looking forward to a time when things will be better. It will just be over and that's all there is to it.

Pastor Anders came to talk to me about it months back. I know he meant to be helpful, and I guess in a way he was, but it's hard to listen to someone talking about the next life when this is the only life you actually know anything about. I believe there's a heaven and everything, but there's nothing familiar in the idea.

The best part of Pastor's visit was when he prayed with me. He just asked God to give me and my family strength and peace. His voice got all quiet and sincere when he prayed and I could tell that he really meant what he was saying.

I rested for a while after the hallway incident and felt a little better by the middle of the afternoon. Momma told me Josie had phoned but I didn't feel like putting on a cheerful face for her, so I didn't bother calling her back right then.

Sitting in the kitchen with Momma, chewing on a piece of whole wheat toast, I remembered about Maryanne.

"I invited Maryanne Richards for dinner tomorrow evening, Momma," I said between bites. "I hope that's okay."

"Tomorrow is fine dear," she answered right away. "Is there anything in particular you'd like me to make?"

I was about to say lasagna, when it occurred to me that Maryanne probably didn't eat too much pasta, especially the way Momma makes it, all loaded with cheese.

"Something low fat, I guess," I decided. "Maryanne has been on a diet for a while."

"In that case, I'll make the chicken and rice casserole you like so much," she answered without commenting on the diet thing or asking any questions.

I thought it would be a good idea to mention how much weight Maryanne had lost anyway. It would be awkward if she came to the door and whoever answered it didn't recognize her. Momma seemed pleased to hear how much Maryanne had changed.

With that taken care of, I thought it would be a good time to go and visit Randy. I was hoping that no one else would be there, but mostly I was hoping that he'd bring up the subject of, well, of *us*, again. This time I'd be ready.

I started out for the jail and would have been there long before dinner if I hadn't run into Mrs. Wickholm on my way.

"Kate!" Her voice had the usual air of snobbery. "Kate Benchworth. Come here for a moment."

"Yes, ma'am?" I felt the irritation that I always experience around her rising in me.

"I was just looking for someone to give me a hand carrying some parcels to my vehicle. Can you spare a few moments?"

I couldn't see any way to avoid helping her without being rude, so I took two of the bags she was holding (parcels indeed!) and followed her along the street to her *vehicle.*

"Thank you, Kate." She lowered her substantial form into the car, adding, "You're a good girl."

Then, right out of the clear blue, Mrs. Wickholm started to cry.

I hardly knew what to say or do. It was just so odd to see the town's grand lady with tears running down her face. Finally I managed a weak, "Are you all right, ma'am?"

She reached her hand out of the car and touched my arm, saying, "I've always thought everything could be solved with money, but it can't."

"No, ma'am." I had no idea what she was talking about. And on top of wanting to get away from her so I could go see Randy, I felt awkward standing there.

It couldn't have been more than a moment or two, although it felt like much longer, until she sniffed loudly, thanked me again, and drove off. I watched with relief as her car disappeared down the street and then continued on my way.

Officer Peterson was at the station when I arrived. He looked up from some kind of form he was filling out and I could tell he was going to ask me all the questions adults sometimes ask kids. Sure enough, he inquired after my folks, asked how I was feeling, what grade I was going into in the fall, and a few of the other usual things. I answered politely, although I've never liked that sort of conversation. You can always tell if someone is asking you questions because they're genuinely interested or if they're just doing it out of a sense of obligation.

He ended our little talk by booming cheerfully, "Well, you take care of yourself now, Kate," and going back to filling out his form.

Randy was standing with a big smile on his face when I reached the cell. He must have heard the conversation down the hallway and been amused to think of me trapped in that kind of boring adult conversation.

"Hey," he greeted me warmly, "I've been waiting impatiently for you to get here."

"Patience is a virtue," I pointed out. "Perhaps you need to work on that."

"It's hard to be patient when you're waiting for someone special."

And then, after all my rehearsing and practicing, there I was all tongue-tied again. I could hardly believe it. I've always been able to ramble on and on. But something about being around Randy turns me into a dolt without a voice.

With relief, I realized that he was speaking again. At least one of us could talk.

"Ma was up earlier today, so we should be able to have a visit without interruptions."

"Your mom is a nice woman," was the best I could come up with by way of an answer. I felt like a complete idiot.

"She's had a hard life, with my pa having a drinking problem and all."

"How does she like working for Mrs. Wickholm?" I asked, remembering the scene on the street a short while ago.

"She likes it a lot." His answer surprised me. "Mrs. Wickholm was very kind to have given her a job when her situation was so desperate. And she's good to my ma."

"I'm glad things worked out for your mom."

"Me too. It looks as though we'll be making our home in Farrago because of this whole thing. I'm not sorry about it either, except for having lost the farm and everything. This is a nice enough place, and the people are good-hearted."

I'd been under the impression that the arrangement for Randy's mom was a temporary one, and that they'd probably be moving along once he was free again. My heart leapt to hear him say they were staying.

"And where will you live, once you're out of here?"

"Mrs. Wickholm has offered me and my ma a permanent spot. She's going to fix up the apartment over the garage for us. Ma will get a full wage for her work, and I'll do odd jobs to pay for the rent of the place."

I suddenly found myself feeling a whole lot more kindly toward Mrs. Wickholm. For years I'd been used to thinking of her as nothing more than a snob who walked around town putting on airs. Now I saw her in a different light altogether.

"I sure like you, Kate."

He'd said it outright, there in the middle of a conversation about other things, like he had been trying to get up the nerve and just had to blurt it out once he felt brave enough.

I drew a deep breath.

"I sure like you right back, Randy," I managed. My voice sounded unnaturally deep or something, but he didn't seem to notice.

"Will you wait for me?" He blushed at that, and added, "I mean, will you be my girl, and not see other guys until I'm out of here and can be a real boyfriend to you?"

Would I wait for him! I nodded happily. There were tears filling up my eyes and he must have noticed because he reached his hand out and brushed my cheek softly, wiping a tear off.

Then he was leaning down and toward me and I knew he was going to kiss me. My legs went all rubbery and weak, but I leaned forward too until we were face to face. His lips touched against mine for just a second or two and something like a sharp shock ran all through me.

And that's how it happened that there in the Farrago police station, I got my first kiss ever.

There was only one thing that kept it from being perfect.

CHAPTER EIGHTEEN

I left the jail that day pretty much walking on cloud nine, and trying to shake the one nagging thought that threatened to ruin everything. It wasn't possible though, and the more I tried to pretend I could just ignore it, the more I knew I couldn't.

I was going to have to tell Randy the truth. Fear filled me, wondering how he might react to the news of my illness. Would he be angry that I hadn't told him right up front? Or would it frighten him and drive him away? It's not exactly something most guys have to deal with — their girlfriends announcing, "Oh, by the way, did I mention I'm dying?"

I'd promised to come back that evening for another visit and I made up my mind on the way home to tell him then. But how? It wasn't going to be easy to just bring it up in the middle of a conversation.

I knew one thing, if I didn't tell him soon, he was bound to hear it from someone else. That would be even worse.

When I got home Momma was just getting the table ready for dinner. I got the silverware and laid it in place as she arranged the plates and cups.

"I was just up to see Randy," I mentioned nonchalantly.

"And how is he today?" Momma kept her voice casual too.

"Fine." I took a deep breath. "Oh, Momma, he asked me if I'd be his girlfriend."

She stopped putting things on the table and turned to me.

"I see. And did you accept him?"

"Yes, but now I have a problem."

"You've not told him about your condition," Momma stated without hesitation.

Astonished at her immediate grasp of the situation, I answered miserably that she was right, and that I had no idea how to broach the subject with him. On top of that, I poured out my concerns as to how he might react once I'd told him.

Momma listened patiently through my torrent of words. "I have found, through the years," she said quietly when I'd finally finished, "that most things are worse when you're worrying about them, than they are when they actually happen. My advice is simply to tell him and see what takes place. There's no point in fretting about it beforehand. If he's as fine a fellow as you apparently think he is, he'll handle it properly."

Somewhat soothed by her words, I managed to eat most of my dinner, though my stomach did occasional flip-flops.

Halfway through our meal, Mark tapped my foot with his under the table.

"I saw you trapped, helping Her Majesty Mrs. Wickholm today." His whisper reached more than me, and Daddy gave him a stern look.

"Speak respectfully of your elders, or don't speak at all," Daddy admonished him. Mark hung his head, but I knew it was out of embarrassment for getting caught and not contrition over his remark.

I found myself telling the family about Mrs. Wickholm's arrangement with Randy and his mother. The sight of her sitting in her car and crying that afternoon kept popping into my head, but I didn't want to mention it in front of Mark. He'd take it and spread it around as a great source of merriment. Now that I knew Mrs. Wickholm was helping Randy's family, I didn't want to betray her.

After supper was over, though, and Momma and I were clearing the table, I found myself telling her about the strange occurrence.

"I didn't know what to do," I finished, "with her sitting there crying and all. What do you suppose could have been wrong with her?"

"Mrs. Wickholm was likely overcome with sadness over you, Kate," Momma said simply.

Impossible! I must have looked as surprised as I felt, for Momma went on to add, "I've seen her weep for you before, dear. In fact, some months back, when the first treatment hadn't cured you, Mrs. Wickholm paid a visit to your father and me."

"What for?" The question came out automatically as I tried to reconcile my lifelong views on her as the town snob with this new information.

"She came to ask if there was any other treatment that might help. And to offer to pay for it. When I told her that the doctor had said there was nothing further that could be done, she wept openly. Oh, I know she has her ways, and sometimes gives people a very bad impression of herself, but she has another side to her too." With a short pause, Momma added, "Most people do."

I stood there feeling very guilty and miserable for all the things I'd thought of Mrs. Wickholm over the years. It had never occurred to me that she was actually kind-hearted. But here she was, helping Randy and his mom, and now I discovered that she had offered to pay for treatment to help me, and cried when she found out there was nothing she could do. It was almost more than I could take in.

It's easier to judge people on what you see, than to look deeper. I have to admit that this wasn't even the first time I'd learned this lesson.

I remember in the first grade there was this boy named Ricky who just basically disgusted everyone. He was always mean and even stole things from other kids' lunch bags. At recess, when the other kids were whooping and hollering, playing in the schoolyard, he would just stand off by himself. Sometimes he'd get into scraps with the other boys, but not often because he was tough and usually won.

But one afternoon during the summer, I'd taken a walk down through the woods near the river. Who did I see there, crouched down along the path, but Ricky. I almost turned to go the other way to avoid him when I realized he was holding a small bird in his hands.

He hadn't heard me coming yet, and I stood stock-still and watched for a moment, wondering what he was up to. Then I heard him talking.

"Hey, little guy," he said, "how'd you get hurt? Well, don't you worry, I'll take you home and take good care of you. You'll be flying again in no time."

His voice was so soft and kind that I almost thought I must be dreaming. Ricky, the obnoxious, hateful kid whom everyone stayed as far away from as possible, all caring and nice to an injured bird. He'd have been the last person I'd have expected to show compassion to anyone or anything. But here was proof that what I'd seen of him wasn't the whole story.

When he'd sensed my presence and discovered he was being watched, his voice and expression changed right away. He stood up, still cradling the helpless little creature in his hands, and faced me with a look of defiance. I knew he was embarrassed that I'd seen the other side of him, so I acted like there was nothing out of the ordinary.

"Hi, Ricky," I said, as though it was normal to speak to him. "I guess that bird is awful lucky you came along. Poor thing."

He let me look at it closer then, but didn't say much and soon headed off home. When school went back in that fall, I had a different attitude toward him, although he still acted the same on the playground. One afternoon around the middle of September, I happened to pass near him in the hallway. Since no one else was around, I stopped and asked him how the bird was.

"Died," he said shortly. "Anyway, it was just a stupid bird."

"I'm real sorry to hear that," I said, ignoring his act, "I know you took care of it as good as anyone could have."

He just stared at me, then walked off, but after that I always said hello to him when I had a chance, and he always answered without any meanness in his voice.

Thinking of all this, I wondered what had become of Ricky. His family had moved away the next year. Well, actually, he and his mom had moved, leaving his father behind on their small dairy farm. The town people said he was an odd man, and that he used to sit his family down and preach strange sermons to them. It was rumoured that after he was left alone, he used to preach to the animals in the barn, but in Farrago you never know if that kind of story is true or not.

I hoped that Ricky and his mom had happier lives now, and that he wasn't angry all the time anymore.

By the time I'd thought all this through, I'd finished clearing the table and was ready to leave. Mark was helping Momma with the dishes and I could hear him singing away, which always amused me. Since Momma often sang doing housework, Mark seemed to think it was an expected thing. From the time he was small, he'd sing tidying up his room, or doing little chores like dusting or sweeping. We usually had to go behind him and do his chores over when he wasn't looking, but Momma said it was important for children to learn responsibility right off.

I guess she was right about that, because Josie and her brother Reggie never helped out at their house when they were smaller, and now they act like it's a crime if someone asks them to do something. Their mom yells at them to clean their rooms some-times, but mostly she does it for them. I guess Josie and Reggie will get an awful shock when they have their own places someday, and have to start doing all the stuff they never had to do before. It takes a lot of work to keep a place clean, which will be a rude dis-covery for them. I'm pretty sure they think it just happens magically.

I grabbed a sweater from my room and threw it over my shoulder since the evenings have been cooler this week. When I got to the bottom of the stairs and headed for the door, Momma popped her head out of the kitchen.

"Good luck, dear," she said giving me a wave.

"Thanks, Momma." And I was off.

The walk to the jail isn't very long, but some days when I was going to see Randy it seemed to take forev-er. Not today. I was there before I knew it. All the way along I'd been thinking of how to bring up the subject of my illness, but nothing seemed quite right. I almost turned around and went back home, but at the last I gathered my courage and headed up the stairs.

I was hoping with all my might that Officer Peterson wouldn't be there tonight, and was relieved to see Officer Johnson at the desk. Even though he was kind of moody at times, which I think had something to do with being newly married, I preferred him because he didn't bother with much small talk.

Sure enough, he just gave me a quick wave and I went straight down the hallway.

Randy was there, standing and waiting for me. A smile lit up his face as soon as he saw me, and I did my best to smile back as naturally as I could.

Little did he know what I was about to tell him.

CHAPTER NINETEEN

The second I came into view, Randy opened his arms, as though he could hug me through the bars, and said, "There's my girl."

I remembered that he'd called me his girl once before, but he hadn't meant the same thing then, at least not as far as I knew. A shiver of happiness tingled through me, and when he reached his hand out through the opening where we'd kissed earlier it seemed the most natural thing in the world to give him mine to hold.

His face got solemn for a second and he commented that he wished he wasn't there, stuck in a jail cell.

"I'd put my arms around you and kiss you properly if I could," he lamented. "But the officer on duty told me there should be a bail hearing later this week. He said it's possible that they'll let me out on my own recognizance until the trial."

"What does that mean?" I felt a surge of joy at the thought of Randy being out of this place.

"Something like on my honour I think," he answered. "Like I promise to show up for court and not get into any more trouble in the meantime."

"Officer Johnson said that might happen?"

"He just said it was possible. But he also told me that the police officers would give statements that I'd been a model prisoner," the words made him stop and smile ruefully before he went on, "and my mom could testify and stuff too."

"What happens if the judge doesn't agree to it?"

"In that case I guess I'm stuck here until I go to trial. And that could be months from now."

"Well, let's pray that it works out for you." I felt ill at the thought of months passing before Randy was out of this place, especially since I could be stuck in a hospital by then. Or worse.

"If it doesn't, I know I have no right to hold you to your promise to wait for me," he said miserably. "I'm sure there are lots of guys who would like to have you as their girlfriend."

"There aren't, but even if there were, it wouldn't matter," I assured him. Deep breath. "There's something I should have told you about long ago."

I held onto his hand tightly and looked directly into his eyes. I could see he was waiting for me to finish what I'd started saying, and I wished I hadn't brought it up already. It could have waited until I was almost ready to leave, until we'd had a nice visit.

"I have a brain tumour," I plunged in, "called an Optic Chiasma. The doctors did radiation and chemotherapy, but they couldn't operate because of where it is."

I stopped to let my words sink in. It was pretty obvious no one had already mentioned it to Randy, because he got a bewildered look, as though I had told him something that just didn't make any sense.

"You're going to be all right, though, aren't you?" he said, when he'd finally found his voice.

"No, I'm not. I'm going to die." There! It was out, and a sense of relief flooded over me. No matter what happened now, at least the hard part of telling him was over.

"But ..." his voice trailed off in disbelief.

"I'm sorry for not telling you before." He was staring at me horrified, and his reaction made me all cold inside. Did he think it was something he could catch, like some of the kids who avoided me like the plague ever since I'd been diagnosed apparently believed?

"When ... I mean," he paused, trying to phrase the question, and finally just asked, "How long?"

"No one really knows," I answered. "It could be a long time yet, or very soon. It depends on how rapidly the tumour grows."

"Does it hurt?"

"Not really, though sometimes I get headaches, or dizzy, or sick to my stomach."

He got silent then for a few moments, just looking back and forth from my face to the floor. I knew he was uncomfortable, but heck, I was uncomfortable too. It was just that there seemed nothing to add to the conversation until he spoke.

I steeled myself for the likelihood that he'd tell me that this changed everything. Even though that was the last thing I wanted to hear, I was determined to handle it without crying. After all, it was my fault for not telling him earlier. If he couldn't face the circumstances, I wasn't about to show my disappointment, or try to persuade him otherwise. At least I could hang onto my dignity.

And then, at last, he lifted his head and looked directly into my eyes. I could see that his own were filling with tears.

"This is hard. This is really hard."

"I know it is. I know it's not fair to you," I managed, dreading the worst but ready to face it.

"Not fair to *me*?!" His voice came out almost as a yell and it startled me so much that I jerked my hand back, away from his. "What are you talking about? *You're* the one who has to go through this."

"But," I stammered, "if we're a couple, it means you have to deal with a lot of stuff too. It was wrong of me to agree to be your girlfriend when I hadn't told you. I mean, you didn't know all the facts when you asked me."

"And you think that would have made a difference?"

"Well, sure. Doesn't it?"

Before he could answer, our attention was drawn to the corner of the hallway, where Officer Johnson's head was poking inquisitively. He cleared his throat in embarrassment.

"I heard yelling," he explained, "so I thought I'd better check to see if everything was all right."

"Sorry, officer," Randy said quickly. "We were discussing something important and I guess I got a little carried away. I'll keep it down."

"No, no, that's fine. Just checking things out. So everything's fine then. Great then, that's just fine. Sorry for disturbing you young folks." He was still apologizing and repeating that everything was fine as he retreated back to the office.

We both giggled, more relieved at the unexpected release of tension than actually amused.

"Listen," I said, "you don't have to, I mean, I don't want you to feel that you should …"

I couldn't finish though, mainly because what I was trying to say was an out and out lie. It didn't matter. Randy beckoned me a bit closer.

I stepped forward as he reached his hand out and circled the back of my head, drawing me toward him.

I thought he was going to kiss me, which would have been perfectly all right with me, but that's not what he did.

Instead, he drew my face up against his, so we were standing cheek to cheek. I closed my eyes and pretty much held my breath, still not sure which way this was going to go. After all, if he was about to dump me, he might be trying to soften the blow by being sympathetic and gentle.

"I don't know how this is going to work out," he spoke at last.

My heart sank, and I couldn't say anything back in spite of my determination to let him go without showing that it hurt me. I managed a tiny nod.

"I mean, think about it. This must be the weirdest relationship in history." His hand squeezed lightly against my head. "Here I am in jail, and there you are, ill. It seems that everything in the world is against us being together."

I swallowed hard and blinked to keep the tears from coming.

"And still, with all that, I've never met anyone in my whole life who I wanted to be with so much, or felt this way about."

And then, of all the crazy things, I *did* cry. I couldn't even tell you *why*! After all, this was exactly what I'd wanted and hoped for, but I still bawled like a baby and hardly had the sense or strength or whatever I should still have had to even feel embarrassed.

Randy was great, though. He didn't shush me or anything, just kept his face pressed against mine until all the tears had drained out of me. That took a while, because there were a lot.

Then, we settled into a long talk then about my illness and how it related to us as a couple. He seemed to be dealing with it much better than I'd expected, although I knew it was still a shock to him and he'd need time for it to fully sink in.

I remember how long it took me to even *begin* to come to terms with the whole thing. It's different to hear something and understand it, and quite another to take it in emotionally. I knew it would be that way for Randy too, that he'd need time to adjust to the idea.

As we talked I wondered briefly what it would be like if it was the other way around, and he'd just told me he was dying. How would I feel and react? It was the kind of juxtaposition that had no answer, and I soon gave up.

It had all been a very emotional thing and before very long I found myself getting really tired. Still, I didn't want to leave. I wished I could stay there forever with him holding my hand and talking in his gentle way. Having my hand resting in his gave me a safe, happy feeling, the kind of feeling you wish would never end.

I tried to push aside thoughts of how drained I felt, just to prolong the evening, but it didn't take long for Randy to see it.

"Kate! You're exhausted, aren't you?" he said suddenly, a frown creasing his forehead. "Here I am jabbering away and you look like you're about to pass out."

"I am kind of tired," I admitted, "but it's so nice being with you that I hate to go."

"And I hate to see you go. Every time you disappear down the hallway, I get a lonely feeling. But I can see that you need some rest."

I gave in without much resistance. The thought of being in my own soft bed was quickly becoming almost as appealing as staying with Randy.

He kissed me then. His lips touched mine and he kept them there for what must have only been seconds but seemed a long time. They just lingered there all soft, and I could feel the warmth of them all the way home.

The walk seemed to take forever, and by the time I rounded the corner to my house I almost felt that I might not make it. It took every bit of strength I had to climb the stairs.

I fell into bed without bothering to change into my nightclothes.

Several hours later I woke, feeling mildly sick. The moon was shining in, making long shadows through the room. Usually, I lie and look at the shadows in the room, making a game out of deciphering strange shapes, which can look spooky until you realize they're just shirts tossed over a chair, or other common things.

This night there were no peculiar shadows or shapes, or if there were I didn't notice them. I rolled out of bed and made my way shakily down the hall to the bathroom. Nausea rolled over me again, but by putting my head down, breathing slowly and evenly, and then washing my face with a cold cloth, it receded.

The thought pushed into my head that it won't be very long now before the end comes. It sent a chill through me, which I fought off by clenching my teeth very hard and forcing the idea away. I told myself the premonition was wrong. I promised myself at least a few more years.

It was all very strange, because I was angry, and yet it seemed as though the anger was directed at me, which didn't make any sense at all.

Chapter Twenty

I slept almost until ten o'clock the next morning and felt a little woozy when I woke up. The first thing I thought of was Randy's kiss and our conversation the evening before. I lay there in bed, waiting to feel a little better before getting up, and, well, I did something kind of silly.

I kissed my hand, pretending I was kissing him again. Then I laughed at myself and wondered if anyone else ever did dumb things like that.

The second thing that popped into my head was that this was the night Maryanne was coming for dinner. I wondered if she was feeling nervous about it, since it would be her first time to see anyone, except for me, in years.

I guess if I'd been a recluse for that long, I'd be pretty anxious about the whole thing. I was glad that it was my house she was coming to, because I knew that Momma and Daddy would make her feel welcome and comfortable.

Once word gets around it will be easier for her, but I know a lot of people will still stare and whisper, especially since Jeff has been in town. I guess I'm not really that much different from the gossips and busybodies, though, because I'm really curious about what happened when Maryanne saw Jeff.

When I went downstairs Momma was busy in the kitchen. I offered to help since I knew she was getting things ready for Maryanne, and after all, I'd invited her, but Momma said she was already ahead of schedule.

"Thanks for having her over," I thought to remark as I was getting an orange out of the fridge. "You're a great mom."

She smiled and hugged me. "You're a great daughter too."

I suddenly got thinking about how she'd mentioned about having a talk to me about boys, and even though I wasn't exactly keen on the idea, I thought it might be something that was important to her. After all, I was the only daughter she had, and she wasn't going to get many chances for that kind of mother-daughter talk. It would be sad for her to look back someday and regret that she'd missed out on giving me dating advice.

So I decided to bring it up, and when I saw the look on her face I was really glad I did. She just seemed so pleased that I was asking for her guidance. I guess that means a lot to parents, to have their kids show an interest in their opinions.

She wiped her hands on a tea towel and sat down at the table, patting the chair beside her. I joined her and found that I was actually feeling curious about what she might have to say on the subject.

"I guess that the main thing I wanted to talk to you about was feelings, Kate."

That surprised me right off. I thought she was going to say something along the lines of the lecture Josie's mom gave to her last year when Josie started to get curves.

Josie and I had giggled ourselves nearly sick the next day, when she told me about it.

"It all started out with Mom telling me she had something important to say." Josie had rolled her eyes, remembering. "She was red in the face before she even started, and when she'd made her speech she looked so happy it was over that I thought she might collapse from relief."

I could picture Mrs. Spencer all flustered, giving the obligatory speech, and the enactment that Josie did fit the idea perfectly.

"Now, Josie. You don't let boys touch you." Josie had mimicked her mom's high-pitched voice perfectly, standing in front of me with one hand on a hip and her eyes looking right straight up at the ceiling.

"Boys want one thing, and one thing only," she shuddered, her lips pursed distastefully. "If you're foolish enough to give it to them, they just run back to their friends and brag, and you never see them again."

We'd agreed that her mom had probably meant well. Either that or she was trying to scare Josie, which I thought was more likely but didn't want to say. For sure she was way off the mark in her assessment of what boys were like. Oh, I know the way things are, don't get me wrong. Some guys are like that all right, but most of them are okay.

Momma didn't have that attitude at all. She seemed calm and comfortable, and acted as though this was something she wanted to tell me.

"Teenagers have so many feelings going on in them that sometimes it's hard to sort them all out. It can be wonderful to care about someone and to have that person care about you too."

I found myself nodding in agreement because it felt really great to like Randy and know he liked me right back. Momma noticed my head bobbing up and down and smiled.

"I see that you're very taken with this young man, and from what I hear, he seems to feel the same way about you. I just want to caution you to take things slowly. Be careful that you know him well before you give him your whole heart.

"Caring about someone can be painful if you find out too late that the person is not what you thought. When you start out dating someone, both of you are going to show your best side, but that doesn't go on forever. None of us are perfect, and sooner or later we find out that the person we're dating has faults, things we just don't like. And they discover the same thing about us as they get to know the things we keep hidden in the beginning."

I already knew that was true from different friendships I'd had over the years. Sometimes friends were great at the start, but as you got to know them better you found out that you weren't really all that crazy about them. Like Amy, a girl I was friends with last year. She had seemed so nice at the start, but I found out that she had a bad habit of talking about other people. It wasn't very long before I realized she was talking behind my back the same way.

It seemed impossible to me, though, that Randy wasn't as wonderful as he seemed. I'd never met anyone as nice or as smart as him before.

"Take your time," Momma continued. "Enjoy dating Randy, but be sure that you get to know him before you get too close. People make the mistake all the time of letting their emotions get deeply involved before they really know much about the person they're seeing. Then it's easier to ignore problems or make excuses for faults than it is to break up."

All of a sudden I knew *exactly* what Momma was

talking about. Right away I got thinking about Julie Sheppard, a girl in the grade ahead of me. She started going out with Paul Maloney when he moved to town last semester, and she was right crazy over him from the very start. All she talked about was Paul, Paul, Paul.

It wasn't very long, though, before everyone knew that Paul didn't treat Julie very nice. It was kind of embarrassing to see her with him because she would just be doing everything possible to please him and he'd be acting like she was of no importance to him at all.

He was rude to her in front of people, and the worse he treated her the more she made excuses for him. She'd say things like, "He's just having a bad day," or "He doesn't really mean it." Even worse was when *she'd* take the blame for his creepy actions and make remarks like, "I shouldn't have done that, I know he doesn't like it."

Eventually, they stopped going out, but the weird thing was that it was Paul and not Julie who broke up, and she cried about it for ages. I couldn't understand any of it until right there at that moment in the kitchen listening to Momma. The way she had just explained things, I could see how Julie had ended up in that situation. She'd let herself like Paul a whole lot, and by the time he started acting like a jerk, she was too far gone to see it.

I wondered if Julie had anyone who took the time to talk about things the way my mother did with me. Maybe she wouldn't have gotten into the whole humiliating mess if she'd had all this stuff explained to her.

I realized then that Momma was sitting quietly, waiting for some kind of reaction from me. And I got this huge feeling of love for her, for how she cared for me so well and what a good mother she really is.

"Thank you, Momma." I went around the table, hugged her tight, and kissed her on the cheek. "I'll remember what you said."

She hugged me back with her eyes all full of tears, but I knew they were happy tears. Then she said, "I just don't ever want to see you hurt, Kate."

I knew what she meant. With the tumour and everything, she wanted to make sure that I didn't have anything else bad in my life.

"I know that, Momma," I said. My voice sounded funny, kind of squeezed, but neither of us laughed about it.

A little while later I decided to head out for a walk and maybe stop by the jail before Maryanne came for supper. Before I left the house I thought it was time to mention something to my mother that I hadn't told her for a long time.

She was in the laundry room, sorting clothes into the washer. She looked up when she noticed me standing in the doorway.

"I'm going for a walk," I said casually. "And Momma, I really love you a lot."

Chapter Twenty-One

I headed out of the house with no particular thought of where I was going, and just walked along aimlessly until I realized I was getting near to Josie's place.

A pang of guilt crept into me when I thought of how little time I'd been spending with her lately. Now that the whole thing with Randy was cleared up, I felt terrible over how easily I'd been willing to think the worst of her.

So, I turned up the walk to her front door and rang the bell. Mrs. Spencer answered the door. A flicker of alarm sped across her face, chased away by a quick, extra-bright smile.

I said good afternoon and asked if Josie was home, keenly aware that she was uncomfortable around me. Sometimes she asks me how I'm feeling in a way that's so sad and sympathetic sounding I can hardly stand it. It really bugs me when someone who never makes any particular effort to find out how I am at any other time acts all caring and concerned if I just happen to be around at the moment.

"Josie's not here right now, dear." She tilted her head, as if the details on Josie's whereabouts were stuck in there and needed a bit of dislodging. "I think she said something about going to Parker's place, but she should be home soon if you want to check back in an hour or so."

"Okay, well, thanks a lot. Tell Josie she can give me a call when she gets home." I blurted the words out as fast as I could, turning and starting to leave at the same time, so as to avoid her insincere inquiries into my health.

It occurred to me a few moments later that maybe I wasn't being fair about Mrs. Spencer, just as I'd been wrong about Mrs. Wickholm. It could be that there was another side to her, a side I hadn't seen. Or maybe she was just the type who doesn't quite know what to say, and comes across as phony because she tries so hard.

It's not like any of us ever *really* know what's going on in someone else's head.

I kept on my walk, not really feeling up to going all the way to the jail right then, even though I'd have liked to see Randy. A few streets later I found myself stopped in front of our little church.

I've always liked our church. It's nestled among a grove of oak trees, a quaint little white building whose stained glass windows create a warm, friendly look, as though it's welcoming you there. I walked past the church and through the parking area behind it, and then crossed the grass to the graveyard.

I used to spend a lot of time in the graveyard when I was a couple of years younger. There was something compelling about it, the quiet and peaceful feeling there, and some of the old stones had interesting things on them.

I went across to one that I'd discovered on my very first trip there, and stood rereading it even though I knew it by heart. The inscription had intrigued me right from the start, but now its meaning was suddenly more real:

Bethany Bannock
beloved daughter
1912–1923
Remember me as you pass by
As you are now, so once was I
As I am now, so you shall be
Prepare for death, and follow me.

A chill went up my back and I sank down to my knees and then found myself folded in half. I wanted to cry, but tears wouldn't come.

As you are now, so once was I … How true those words were. This girl, who had lived only eleven years, had once lived and breathed just like me.

As I am now, so you shall be ... I shuddered.

The stillness of the cemetery suddenly bothered me in a way it never had before. Its silence no longer seemed tranquil, but ominous. I wondered why I'd ever thought of the quiet as a peaceful thing, instead of what it really was — evidence of death. The graveyard's silence was created because its cold inhabitants no longer had breath to speak.

As I am now, so you shall be. A low moan rose in my chest, startling me for a second until I realized it was coming from me.

When? When would I be cold and still, just like that girl lying there all these years?

"If I could just have a few more years," I heard myself say, my voice a choked, pleading whisper. "Three years. I'd never do anything wrong, ever again. I'd be so good, and see the best in everyone. Even two years. Two years would be enough. Just to do a few of the things I want to do. Not all of them — just some. If I could even have one more whole year...."

I realized after a moment that I was praying. Well, in a way. I used to listen to some of the older folks pray at church meetings, and think of how some prayers are nothing more than long lists of requests. Mine was closer to a combination of begging and bargaining, but I couldn't help myself from asking for what my whole heart wanted. The only thing in the world that mattered to me. Time.

Then it seemed as though I collapsed inward, as

though everything crushed toward the inside of me and pushed harder and harder until my whole self was a tight, hard ball in the centre of my chest. It hurt so much I could hardly breathe, but I knew it wasn't because of my illness.

I got back to my feet unsteadily and began to run, wanting to be out of there, wanting to forget that in a very short time I too would be among those buried in that very place.

As I hurried past the church I heard a voice calling my name. When I turned, I saw Pastor Anders standing on the steps.

He walked quickly toward me, and I saw from the expression on his face that he'd witnessed at least some of what had just happened in the graveyard.

When he reached me, he put his arm around my shoulders and led me silently over to the low stone wall that borders the edge of the lawn.

As we seated ourselves there he began to speak.

"You know, Kate, it's okay to cry. We have emotions for a reason."

"I do cry sometimes," I told him, "but there are times when I don't want to think about it anymore. Only I can never get away from it. It's there every minute of every day."

"It's a heavy burden for such a young person," he said softly. "Be sure you're not trying to carry it all by yourself."

I thought then that he was going to talk about faith and trust but instead he started talking about all the people we have in our lives who love us.

"Love comes from God," he told me, "and the power of love is greater than we can ever understand. It gives us strength and courage to face things that we could never face alone."

Then he said a prayer with me, a simple prayer asking for peace and comfort for me and for all those who love me.

"You're not alone here," he said quietly, "and you won't be alone when you cross over to the next life."

I thought about that on the way home, and about how many people I have who really, truly love me. My family first, of course, but others too. Suddenly I could almost feel a force surrounding me, even though I was still walking alone. It was like a hundred arms around me, holding me. It gave me a feeling of happiness that I can't remember ever feeling before. It floated through me, washed over me, and filled me all at once.

"Please, just let me *live* every moment that I have left," I said. I almost went on, as if God needed me to explain exactly what I meant. I didn't bow my head or close my eyes, but I think it was the truest prayer I ever made.

I guess it was at that moment that I really accepted what lies ahead.

Chapter Twenty-Two

After leaving the graveyard I meandered up and down the streets for a while. My thoughts soon turned to Maryanne and I decided to go to her house to see if she wanted to walk to my place with me. I figured that she was probably nervous about being seen on the street by herself, seeing as she hadn't been anywhere during the daytime for so long.

I was almost to her street when I saw Mark's familiar figure heading toward me. He had a searching look on his face, the way you get when you're looking really hard for someone or something, and you almost don't see anything else around you because of it. When he saw me coming along his face lit up with an expression that said "there she is" as clearly as if he'd said it aloud.

I realized with a sudden little pain that we hadn't spent much time together the past few weeks and felt immediate remorse at having neglected him. I'd been so busy with my own concerns that Mark had sort of gotten put to the side.

His voice was casual enough when he called out, "Hey, Kate!" but the nonchalance of his words was belied by his eager expression.

"Hey, squirt," I answered, ruffling his hair as we reached each other. "Whatcha up to?"

"Nuthin." He looked as though he wanted to say more, but just stood there, shuffling his feet back and forth on the sidewalk.

"Me neither." I found myself almost lost for a few seconds, looking at him, just a little boy who must have a lot going on inside that he never talked about. "Come on, let's go for a walk."

We fell into step in a comfortable silence for a short while, and I was trying to think of how to get a conversation going when he spoke.

"You haven't been feeling very good, have you?"

"I get dizzy sometimes, and sick to my stomach," I answered truthfully, "but most of the time I feel okay. It's not so bad, really."

He absorbed this before saying, "You're going to feel worse and worse though, aren't you?"

"I guess I'll get sicker," I allowed, "but the doctor will put me in the hospital then, and they'll give me medicine and stuff to keep me from feeling too bad."

"Justin's brother was sick for a while," Mark said, his tone so hollow that it almost sounded as though he was speaking from a long distance away. "But they did some kind of operation and took something out and he's okay now."

"An appendectomy," I told him. "Justin's brother had appendicitis so they had to remove it to make him better."

"I wish they could do something like that for you." His voice sounded tiny and forlorn.

My chest got all tight and achy when he said that, and I could hardly keep tears from coming to my eyes. All I could do was squeeze out the words, "I know you do, kid, but they can't always remove things that make people sick."

It seemed that he kind of sagged after that, like a beach ball that's had some air let out.

"Some of my friends have older sisters, and they complain about them all the time."

"That's pretty normal," I answered.

"Not for me," he said earnestly. "We get along good, don't we?"

"Yes, because we're not just brother and sister. We're friends." It was true too. "You're a great brother."

"You're a great sister." He was choking now, on the verge of crying and trying to hold it back.

"Overall, I'd say we're pretty lucky," I told him

softly, putting my arm on his shoulder. "I got to have a brother who's hardly ever annoying, and you got to have a sister who's really cool."

He laughed at that, gurgling chuckles coming up unexpectedly among the tears he was trying to fight down. Within seconds he was laughing and crying at the same time, which I'd heard of but had never seen anyone do before.

"Remember," he gasped between sobs and giggles, "remember that time we planted cucumbers in Mom's flower bed?"

Momma starts a lot of her flowers from seed, early in the spring. A few years ago Mark and I had found a package of cucumber seeds in the shed and stuck them in her flower beds. We hadn't known anything much about plants then and thought it would be a great joke when cucumbers started popping up among the flowers.

A few weeks later at the supper table Momma casually told Daddy that she had dug out a section of ground and made a raised bed along the side of the yard that she didn't use for her flowers.

"Oh?" Daddy wasn't all that interested in Momma's flowers, although he always went to see them when she asked him to, and always said they were "real pretty" and stuff.

"Yes, I have some cucumbers that will have to be transplanted." She never so much as glanced at me or

Mark as she spoke. "Somehow, they've begun growing all on their own right in the midst of my marigolds and pansies."

Daddy looked up, his face all puzzled. "You don't say," he said.

"Yes, it's a real mystery," Momma nodded as though she was just as surprised as he was. "I was thinking that maybe Kate and Mark would like to take care of them."

At first it seemed that the joke was on us, but it turned out to be a really cool thing. We dug up the tiny plants and put them in their new home, which was the first lesson in gardening for us. It became pretty clear how Momma had known the difference from the shape of the leaves, although Mark and I had thought all plants looked pretty much the same until they got flowers on them.

Then we spent hours taking care of them, watering and weeding. Instead of it being like work, it was exciting watching them grow and crawl across the lawn. We learned that they get flowers first, and when the cucumbers came we were as proud as could be.

It had been a great time for Mark and me, working and learning on a project together. Thinking of it now, we began talking about that and other times we'd spent doing things over the years. My head was starting to ache, and dizziness was getting the best of me, but I managed to push the feelings aside enough to continue talking as though nothing was wrong.

Suddenly, Mark made an announcement right in the middle of our talk.

"If I get married and have kids some day, and one of them is a girl, I'm going to call her Kate."

I hugged him hard, there on the street.

Then, wanting to rest for a few minutes without Mark seeing how I felt, I told him I was going to meet Maryanne and walk her to the house for supper. He headed off and I sank down on the curb and put my head between my knees, willing the pain and dizziness to subside.

It seemed a long time before I felt well enough to move again, and when I did, I found my steps were slow and awkward, as though my legs had turned to stone.

When I got to Maryanne's door I was ready for another rest. Thankfully, she invited me in and I sank gratefully down on the couch while she seated herself in a big armchair across from me.

"You look pale, Kate," she observed with genuine concern in her voice.

"I'm not feeling great," I admitted, "but it comes and goes. It will pass if I can just lie down for a bit."

She went off to get me a pillow, which she fluffed before putting under my head. Leaning over me she bent down close and kissed my forehead. I had the feeling that it wasn't the kind of thing that came easily for her, and that made it mean a lot.

The next thing I knew, I was waking up! Blinking and rising up on one elbow I found Maryanne quietly watching me, her face suffused with caring.

"Oh, dear," I smiled weakly, "I guess I was pretty tired."

"You only slept for about half an hour," she answered. "How are you feeling now?"

"Much better, thank you." Remembering our supper plans I asked her what time it was, and she told me she'd called my place and Momma had told her there was no rush, we could eat whenever I woke up and was ready to come.

"Your father will pick us up if you like."

"I think I'd rather walk. It's not very far, and I think some fresh air will do me good."

She agreed, and we headed out. On the way, I asked her how the visit had gone with Jeff.

"It wasn't at all what I expected." She shook her head slowly. Her eyes kind of drifted then, like she wasn't quite there with me. I figured she was reliving some part of what had taken place between them, which only served to increase my curiosity.

"Turns out neither one of us was right about his reason for coming here," she said after a moment. "He wasn't looking for a divorce, as I'd been so sure he was, and even the word 'reconciliation' was never mentioned. Not that I expected it would be."

I thought I heard something in her voice — maybe a twinge of wistfulness or a hint of regret? I couldn't be sure, and there was no way I could ask.

"This town," Maryanne was continuing, "will hate to find out how little drama there really was over Jeff's sudden appearance. The long and the short of it is just this: Jeff came to ask for my forgiveness."

"Your forgiveness?"

"That's right. Well, there's a bit more to it than that. I don't suppose it will hurt to tell you the whole story. You'll keep it between the two of us." She glanced at me and nodded, as though she'd asked me a question and I'd answered it in a way that pleased her. "Apparently, Jeff has had a bit of an affair with the bottle in the years since he left. Trying to avoid his conscience, no doubt.

"Anyway, a few months back it seems he was on the verge of losing his job, and not for the first time either. He went to an organization that helps folks with that sort of problem. Got sobered up, but one of the things they told him he needed to do was make amends for any past wrongdoing. And that's where his visit to me came in."

"And did you forgive him?"

"I told him I did, told him that right off. Then we talked, oh, I imagine it was only for a few minutes, but it seemed a lot longer. You see, I could hardly wait for him to leave."

"How come?"

"Because I was furious, and I didn't want him to see it."

"But I thought you forgave him."

"Well, that's what I said all right. And I tried to mean it. The odd thing is that I hadn't even known I had any bad feelings left toward him. I thought I'd gotten over the whole thing a long time ago. It was a big surprise to discover that wasn't quite true. There must have been a lot of feelings left over, pushed down and hidden. They sure came out this afternoon."

"What happened?"

"Nothing *happened*, really. I just got thinking about all the hurt and humiliation I'd been through over him and it made me very, very angry. Had a bit of a private tantrum, I suppose. And then I think I let go of it. But who knows? There could be more that will surface later."

"Yeah," I agreed. "You never know when feelings will decide to get your attention."

CHAPTER TWENTY-THREE

I was never so proud of my family as I was that night, with Maryanne there for dinner. From the moment she stepped through the door everyone made her feel as welcome as if she was an old family friend.

Momma and Daddy complimented Maryanne on her appearance, but the way they did it was just like something they'd say to anyone who looked nice. I mean, it didn't sound at all like they were saying how much *better* she looked than before, just that she looked really nice, which she did.

Little brothers aren't usually that subtle though, and mine is no exception.

When Mark came into the dining room where we were all seated, he stopped dead in his tracks and stared for a few seconds.

"Wow."

I felt my face getting hot when he managed that single word, but Maryanne started to laugh and then we all joined in and what could have been a tense moment passed.

Mark blushed and stammered an embarrassed hello. Maryanne smiled at him as though he was the most adorable little boy she'd ever seen, and said hello back.

Momma's meal was great and I ate way too much, so that when it was time to clean up and do the dishes, I felt like I could hardly move from the table. It was okay though, because Maryanne insisted on helping Momma with the dishes, and they were out in the kitchen chatting like old friends in no time.

Daddy went off to read the paper while Mark and I watched some television, and before long Momma and Maryanne joined us and settled on the couch with cups of tea. We had just started up a conversation when there was a knock at the door.

Mark went to answer it. Our family has a kind of unspoken hierarchy that says Mark and I get the door and the phone if we're home. I used to think it was because we're younger and it saved Momma and Daddy from getting up, but now I think it's because most of the time phone calls and visitors are for us.

But this night it was Mrs. Wickholm and Mrs. Nichols at the door. Mrs. Wickholm waltzed in like the residing queen, but it didn't bother me the way it used to. Now that I know what she's like inside, I find myself a lot more tolerant of the airs she puts on.

"Oh, do excuse us," she said, putting her purse down and seating herself regally in an empty chair, "I had no idea that you had company."

Mrs. Nichols remained standing in the archway to the living room, looking really uncomfortable with the role of intruder. Momma stood up right away and urged her to have a seat.

Mrs. Wickholm was looking at Maryanne as though she was trying to figure something out, and I almost giggled, knowing that she was thinking she knew who it was but couldn't quite place her.

Momma cleared up the mystery for her when she hastened to make introductions between Maryanne and Mrs. Nichols, who greeted each other politely.

Mrs. Wickholm's eyes got rounder and her mouth formed a little "O" and when she managed to speak it was more a question than anything, even though she'd just been given the answer.

"Maryanne? Maryanne Richards?"

"Hello, Lila." Maryanne looked amused, although a little uncomfortable at the same time.

"Why, I can't believe it. Gracious sakes, I would never have known you. In fact, I was just sitting here thinking you looked familiar, but I would never have figured out who you were if Lillian hadn't introduced you to Irene." Her powers of speech fully recovered, Mrs. Wickholm shifted into high gear.

"Well, dear, I have to say that you look just marvellous. Yes you do. I don't know how you did it, heaven knows I've battled with this extra twenty pounds for years and never quite managed to conquer them. But you, why, you've clearly won the battle and I'm so proud of you, why, I can hardly speak."

It was obvious that Mrs. Wickholm was quite able to speak, despite her last remark.

"How did you do it? You simply *must* tell me your secret. My goodness, I just can't believe what a change it's made in you. How much did you actually lose, dear?"

Momma looked appalled at the question but there was nothing that could be done about it. Everyone was looking at Maryanne now, waiting to see how she'd answer such an impertinent question.

"I never stepped on a set of scales," Maryanne said calmly, "so I can't tell you that. I can tell you that it was enough to make me feel healthy and energetic."

"Well, my goodness, my goodness," Mrs. Wickholm shook her head and then nodded approvingly. "It surely must have been a *lot*! You look just fabulous."

"Actually, Lila," Maryanne seemed unaffected by the rude remark, "the changes were as much from inside as outside. I had a lot of emotional baggage to get rid of at the same time. It was sort of an overall approach."

"Isn't that interesting," Mrs. Wickholm said, managing to look anything but interested. I could see from her face that her mind had moved on to something else, and I almost cringed waiting to see what was coming next.

"Well, it's no wonder then — that your husband is back in town." Mrs. Wickholm's remark made Momma gasp right out loud, but Maryanne continued to appear calm.

"I suppose that's what people will assume," she said mildly, "but actually, Jeff didn't know about any of this until he came to town."

"He's been to see you, though." Mrs. Wickholm leaned forward quizzically and left the remark hanging, waiting on a reply.

"I don't suppose that's any secret in this town," Maryanne acknowledged. I have to admit I felt a flush of pride because I was the only one in the room who had been filled in on the details of Jeff's visit.

"Well, dear, don't keep us in suspense!" Mrs. Wickholm said in her most commanding voice. "What did he want?"

"I think that's Maryanne's business," Momma spoke, finally having had enough of Mrs. Wickholm's rude prying. "She shouldn't be put on the spot like this."

"Oh, Lillian, there are no secrets in Farrago," Mrs. Wickholm said reproachfully, as though Momma was the one breaching all semblance of etiquette. Even so, she seemed to give up the interrogation for the moment.

"I almost forgot why we came over." She perked up at the thought so I knew it must be some sort of news. Mrs. Wickholm is always perkiest when she has news to tell.

"Irene's boy, Randy, is going to have a bail hearing tomorrow. His lawyer says he'll probably be out of that place after that until the trial."

I was surprised to hear that Randy had a lawyer since he hadn't mentioned one to me. But mostly, I was excited to hear that he might be getting out of the jail cell. My pleasure was short-lived though, because Mrs. Wickholm went on to say, "I thought Kate would want to know since she's his girlfriend."

Daddy's eyebrows shot up so fast you'd have thought they were spring-loaded. I tried not to look at him even though I knew he was staring at me. Once again, Momma made an attempt to smooth things over.

"Well, Kate and Randy have developed a nice little friendship," she said mildly. "I'm sure Kate is pleased about his news." Turning to me she added, "In fact, Kate, you should go visit him this evening. I imagine he'd like some company."

Mrs. Nichols hadn't missed the expression on Daddy's face either. "I'm sure he would, Kate," she said, in her quiet way, "he really does appreciate your friendship."

Both women downplaying Mrs. Wickholm's remark seemed to calm Daddy because he shot me one last inquisitive look but then drifted back to the usual half bored and half trapped expression he wore when there were a bunch of women talking in the room around him.

I thought it would be best if I didn't look too eager to go, although, in my mind, my feet were already flying there. So, I stayed for about another twenty minutes. It turned out to be a lucky thing that I did.

My mind had almost floated away from the conversation completely (I admit I was imagining a kiss and hug from Randy with no jail bars between us) but Mrs. Wickholm caught my attention when she managed to insult Momma's new curtains.

"I suppose your new drapes were ordered from the catalogue," she said, looking at them critically. "They're nice enough, I guess, although not the colour I'd have chosen for this room."

"I like them." Momma refused to let Mrs. Wickholm annoy her with her comment. "I wanted something neutral, so when we change colour schemes they'll go with anything."

"Speaking of colour schemes," I interrupted, "you should *see* Maryanne's place! She redecorated it herself, and it's amazing!"

"Is that so?" Mrs. Wickholm was clearly ruffled that it was anyone's house except her own being mentioned so favourably. The few times I've been inside Mrs. Wickholm's house, I've always been struck with the thought that she'd tried unsuccessfully to copy some decorating idea from a magazine.

"In fact, she's going to start a home decorating business." I realized once I'd blurted this out that Maryanne hadn't actually said for sure what she'd decided on the idea. But before I could correct myself, Mrs. Wickholm had turned to Maryanne and was speaking.

"Well, I'd like to have a look at what you've done with your place, since Kate seems so impressed by it. If you're as talented as she says, I'll be your first customer. I'm thinking that I'd like to do over a few rooms in my house."

Maryanne just nodded in agreement, but I could see in her eyes that she was excited at the thought.

"And of course, that would give your business just the start it needs," Mrs. Wickholm added with satisfaction. "I don't like to boast, but I've always been something of a trend-setter around here."

I felt pretty good about how things had turned out as I headed out the door and up the road to see Randy.

When I got there though, we'd barely had time to say hello when I was hit with another headache and wave of nausea.

"I think there's just been too much going on today," I apologized, "I really need to get home to bed."

I could still see the look on his face when I got back to my house and fell into bed. It reminded me of a scene in an old black-and-white movie, when the hero and heroine had known they were to be parted forever, and he was saying goodbye to her, trying to be strong, but looking for all the world like he couldn't bear it.

Chapter Twenty-Four

When I woke up the next morning I felt like a new person. Whether it was the rest or the excitement of knowing that Randy was having a hearing that could set him free, at least temporarily, or a combination of the two, I couldn't say. I only know that I felt great. Until I rolled over and looked at the clock.

"Oh, no," I moaned, sliding my feet out of bed and onto the floor. The bail hearing had been scheduled for nine in the morning and here it was nearly eleven o'clock. I'd missed it completely, although I'd told Randy I'd be there for sure when he'd given me the time last evening.

I washed my face and brushed my teeth and then went downstairs to get a quick snack before showering. I could hear Momma singing quietly in the kitchen, and

Mark laughing in the living room as I descended the steps. I popped into the room to see what was amusing him so much on TV.

I saw that the TV screen was blank grey just before it registered that Mark wasn't alone. Seated beside him on the couch was Randy, looking at me with overt amusement.

"Morning, sleepyhead," he greeted me cheerfully. "I guess the old expression 'I'll see you in court' doesn't apply to you."

"I'm so sorry," I stammered, "I guess I forgot to set my alarm, although I never sleep this late."

"Too bad," he laughed. "You missed out on hearing my mom tell the judge what a grand fellow I really am. I was surprised he didn't give me a medal before he released me, after she was done."

"I assume then, that your mother is given to gross exaggeration."

"No, in fact I think my virtues were somewhat understated," he rejoined.

"Nice outfit you have on, Kate," Mark snickered, joining the conversation.

I blushed, remembering that I was standing there in my pyjamas, and my hair not even combed!

"Oh! I didn't know anyone was here." I felt the red deepen in my cheeks. Darn this fair complexion! I can never hide it when I'm embarrassed.

"I'm glad you didn't," he said. "You're awfully cute like that."

Mark rolled his eyes and made a pretend gagging sound while I scurried back up the stairs.

When I'd showered, dressed, and re-entered the living room about fifteen minutes later Momma had joined Mark and Randy and they were in the middle of a conversation.

"She's been very good to my mother, and to me," Randy was saying.

"She's a big old *snob*," Mark argued, rolling his eyes and making a face.

I knew immediately whom they were talking about and made a mental note to fill Mark in on some of the things I'd learned about Mrs. Wickholm. It would be good for him to discover that what we see in a person isn't necessarily the whole story.

"Now, Mark," Momma corrected him mildly. "You don't speak that way about your elders." I knew she'd have been more severe with him if she wasn't still annoyed at some of the things Mrs. Wickholm had said last evening.

Randy, to my great pleasure, seemed to have lost all interest in the conversation and was, instead, smiling broadly at me.

"What are your plans, now that you're *finally* up and dressed?" he asked teasingly.

"First of all, I'm going to have a nutritious breakfast," I said, "because breakfast is the most important meal of the day."

Momma knew I was being cute, quoting her like that, but she also knew I didn't mean it in a saucy way.

"Very important," Randy agreed solemnly, catching on right away.

"Since it's almost lunchtime, Randy might as well join you, Kate," Momma said. Then she turned toward him and added, "You just make yourself at home and help yourself to anything you'd like for lunch while Kate is getting her breakfast."

"Thank you, ma'am." He got up and headed toward the doorway where I was standing. "I ate just before I came over, but I'll keep Kate company, if that's all right. And I'll try to make sure she eats something important."

When we got into the kitchen I turned to ask Randy something but before I could get the words out of my mouth he leaned down, wrapped his arms around me, pulled me to him, and kissed me. It left me breathless and dizzy, but in a nice way.

"I've been thinking about doing that all morning," he told me. "Even at the hearing it was practically the only thing on my mind."

I couldn't speak. My throat felt strange and tight and I was sure that if I even tried to say something it would come out as a big squeak. The best I could do was give him a lopsided smile and hope I didn't look as awkward as I felt.

I made some breakfast then but could barely eat for the trembling inside me. The whole time I was eating Randy kept stroking my cheek and arm with his hand. There were feelings rushing around inside me that I'd never felt before.

When I'd finished what I could of my food, I went back upstairs to brush my teeth again, and splash some cool water on my face. Relatively composed, I met him at the bottom of the stairs and we told Momma we were going for a walk.

Out on the street, walking along with my hand tucked safely in his, I felt a surge of pride. It's hard to go anywhere in Farrago without people noticing and commenting on it, especially if there's any kind of news involved. Walking with Randy would certainly be news, and it made me feel oddly important.

We hadn't gone two blocks when I saw Josie and Parker coming toward us from the direction of her house. We greeted each other as we met and decided to head down to the river for a walk. I was a little bit disappointed, because I'd wanted Randy all to myself, but at the same time I was glad since I hadn't seen Josie much the past short while.

Along the trail to the river, Randy kept pointing out different kinds of plants and trees and telling us things about them that I hadn't known before.

"This is a Jerusalem Artichoke," he said, pointing to a tall plant with a pretty yellow flower. "The tubers can be eaten in a variety of ways, cooked or sliced raw in salads or even pickled. They have a nice, sweet, nutty flavour. And over here is Lamb's-Quarter, which has a unique and pleasant taste. It's best to boil it, although you can eat a small amount raw."

I was fascinated with his knowledge and looked at each plant with interest, a reaction that was not shared by Josie and Parker. They nodded and said things like "mmmmm hmmmm" and "oh, yes" but never left the trail to peer closely at anything. I had the impression that they felt trapped in an unscheduled biology class, which they would have preferred to avoid.

Suddenly, Randy stopped walking and peered down along a small brook near the trail.

"Omigosh, Kate!" he said excitedly. "Come with me."

He took my hand and led me a few yards along the brook to a cluster of plants growing near its edge. I thought right off that they were a bit too ordinary look-ing for anyone to get that animated over.

"These are touch-me-nots," he explained, "and as ripe as can be."

"Why do they call them touch-me-nots?"

He took my hand and, extending my index finger, reached it out and touched the bottom of one of many fat green pods hanging from the plant. The second my finger touched it there was a tiny explosion as the pod burst apart and seeds flew everywhere.

It startled me the way a jack-in-the-box does when it pops up and we both laughed. I must have spent at least ten minutes touching and exploding pods. Every time one popped open and sent a tiny shower of seeds flying we laughed again.

"This is how a touch-me-not plant spreads," Randy told me. "Animals brush against them, or the wind rustles them enough for the pods to touch leaves around them, and new seeds are sown for the next year."

It was one of the more delightful things I could ever recall doing, standing there alongside a brook with Randy, laughing and enjoying a simple pleasure of nature.

In the meantime, Josie and Parker were getting impatient. We tried to urge them to come and join in the fun, but Josie didn't want to get her shoes damp and Parker said he'd rather stay there with her. Reluctantly, we drew ourselves away from the brook and joined them again on the trail.

By the time we'd reached the river I knew I was going to need to rest for a while. The now all-too-familiar symptoms were returning again, and though I hated to spoil things for the others I knew that if I pushed myself I'd soon be really ill.

It didn't take long for Josie and Parker to get tired of sitting on the riverbank. They told us they were going back to town to play pinball at the arcade and suggested we could meet them there later if we liked.

Randy sat down at my side and stroked my forehead while I lay there waiting for the pain behind my eyes to subside. In no time, I'd drifted off to sleep.

CHAPTER TWENTY-FIVE

Randy was lying at my side with his arm around me when I woke up. At first I thought he was sleeping but as soon as I made a slight movement his eyes opened and he smiled at me.

"Feeling better?"

"I think so. But my throat is a bit dry."

He got up and helped me to my feet, telling me that he'd seen a freshwater spring just off the path a short way back. We walked there slowly, hand in hand. Silence hung around us like a soft, comforting blanket, as though words were unnecessary and even unwelcome at the moment.

I kneeled down by the spring and scooped mouthfuls of water up with my hand. It was cold and clear and unbelievably refreshing. Once my thirst was gone, I splashed water on my face, washing away the lingering sleepiness.

Back on the path, our steps turned automatically toward the riverbank again. As we made our way there, the warm sun and slight breeze soon dried the droplets of water that clung to my face.

We reached the river in a few moments, then walked upstream to a place where a cluster of rocks hangs out over the bank. I've often gone to this spot alone, sitting and thinking and just feeling the peacefulness that always comes from being at the river. There's something about watching the water that nearly hypnotizes me, and leaves me feeling totally calm.

The river was smooth as glass today, broken only by the occasional ripple caused when a fish arched through the air, its return plunge sending out a circle of waves. Toward the centre of the river a pair of ducks floated serenely, their heads dipping down out of sight every so often as they found food.

Randy pointed across the river to a large cluster of branches piled near the end of a stream. I'd seen the stream before, but never noticed the rounded heap of branches there.

"What is it?"

"It's a beaver dam. They build their homes near certain kinds of trees, like poplar, which is their main source of food." I squinted as he spoke, but saw no sign of a beaver.

"They mate for life," he added.

"What if one of them dies?"

"The other one stays alone."

"That's kind of sad."

"I guess once they have the mate that was meant for them they never want another one." He was looking at me when he said this and I felt the meaning of his words in me.

I took a deep breath.

He leaned forward and kissed me, his hand cupping my chin.

"I feel like I found the perfect girl for me, and that there could never be anyone else as special as you." His voice cracked as he spoke. "I know this is going to sound crazy because we've only known each other for a short time, but I love you, Kate."

My heart gave a huge leap when he said that and before I knew what I was saying, out came the words, "I love you too, Randy." As soon as they were out of my mouth I knew they were true. I hadn't even let myself think about it before, the idea of loving him.

It seemed as though it shouldn't have been. It wasn't fair to me, or to him. Soon I'd be gone and he'd be alone.

Of course, he wouldn't *always* be alone. The thought of making him promise that he'd never love anyone else popped into my head. It was pretty tempting, but I knew it would be a stupid (okay, and selfish) thing to say.

People get over things. Randy would move on and find someone else.

"I guess once I'm gone you'll probably find another girlfriend pretty quick," I said, hoping he'd at least tell me it would take a long, long time before he could even look at another girl. You know, 'cause it would be ages before he could even *start* to like someone else.

"Don't talk like that, Kate."

"Well, you *will*. I mean, it's not like it won't happen."

"Stop that." He was frowning, which made him look angry, though his eyes were only sad. "What counts for us is *today* and what happens while we're together. Anything down the road from now, well, it's not even worth thinking about. I love you. And no matter what comes along later in life, that will always be true."

"You'll never forget me?" I knew I was being the hugest baby ever, that I was pushing for him to say things that most guys never have to say — or even think about — and that it wasn't fair or smart. If anything, it was likely to scare him off.

"No, I'll never forget you." Randy smoothed the hair back off my forehead and kissed me there, soft and gentle-like.

"Swear it." Why couldn't I just stop? Why would I even *want* him to carry the unhappy memory of a dead girlfriend around with him for the rest of his life?

"I swear, Kate, I'll never forget you." His eyes seemed to look right into me, as if he could see past all the foolishness of what I was saying, as if he could see right inside to the fear and hurt.

It all came pouring out then, the thoughts I'd been having lately, the bargaining prayer I'd prayed the other day, the longing for more time and the near panic that rose in me as more and more often it seemed the minutes were flying by faster and faster, as though my life had started playing in the wrong speed, and hours had been crushed into seconds.

"Am I babbling?" I asked after he'd sat silently, just listening, for at least twenty minutes while I blurted one thought after another.

"No," he leaned down, kissed the tip of my nose, "you're not babbling. Just keep talking as long as you want. I'm here and I'm not going anywhere."

Of course, seeing as how my emotions were totally out of whack, that remark made me cry. More accurately, I burst into tears and bawled like a little kid throwing a tantrum. Randy just held me. I clutched onto him, and sobbed until there was a big wet spot on his shirt. Well, it might not all have been tears, but what kind of girl wants to admit she kind of slobbered on her boyfriend?

And then, right out of nowhere, I started laughing. Randy must have been pretty perplexed by then, but he just kept holding me and kind of rocking me against him, and eventually, I evened out and the big outburst was over with.

From that moment on, it was the most wonderful day you could imagine. Being with Randy was the closest I've ever felt to pure happiness and contentment. We talked about nothing and everything, walking in the woods, holding hands, kissing and laughing.

It was the kind of day that you never want to see end. I wished there could be a thousand more just like it.

But one perfect day is, after all, better than none.

Chapter Twenty-Six

I don't remember a single thing about getting here, which is kind of disappointing. I always thought that if I was going to be taken somewhere in an ambulance, I'd want to hear the sirens and everything. But whatever amount of excitement was generated by my trip to the hospital, I missed out on it completely.

It amuses me to think of the phone lines buzzing like crazy, everyone wanting to be first to tell the news. "Poor little Kate Benchworth was rushed to the hospital by ambulance today." There'd be a big, sad sigh and then the words, "I guess the end is near. It's so sad."

Well, I guess the end *is* near. All I remember clearly was a blinding headache, the worst I've ever had. I went to my room to lie down but it wasn't getting any better. I tried to go back downstairs to tell Momma I needed something for the pain, but I never got to the bottom.

Well, I guess I *did* get to the bottom since Momma heard a crash and found me crumpled there in a heap, but I don't remember anything about that.

The next thing I knew I was on a stretcher in the hospital and a doctor was leaning down over me. Not my own doctor, mind you, but I knew it was a doctor anyway because she had on one of those long white jackets that they all wear.

"Well," she said sternly, "you gave your mother quite a scare."

It hardly seemed fair, being lectured for something that wasn't my fault. I tried to protest, but the doctor was smiling then and I realized that she was trying to lighten the situation with a joke.

"I'll probably get grounded for it." I managed a weak smile back, but I felt horrible.

The next few days were spent with tests and more tests. My own doctor came in every morning and afternoon. He never said much to me, but I knew what was going on. He wore an expression as if he'd been looking and looking for something really important, and couldn't find it.

He talked to me about more treatments. I told him I'd think about it, and I did. In the end I said no. It wasn't worth all the suffering when it wasn't going to make me better. The most tempting part was the idea that I'd have more time to spend with Randy, but I knew it wouldn't be good time. I feel that there's no point in prolonging this thing.

I think it was the bravest thing in the world for Momma and Daddy to let me make that decision myself. I'm only fourteen and they could have insisted and signed papers, but they talked it over with me and said they'd respect what I wanted.

On the fourth day here I asked Mark to look under my mattress and bring me my journal and some pens. So here I am, sitting in this bed, knowing that I'm not going to be leaving this place, and trying to wrap up the story while I can.

I've written a note in the front of this journal saying that I want it to be given to Randy when I'm gone. I know that he'll be glad to have it, and will do whatever he thinks is best with it. It's cool to be able to trust someone so much, even though I haven't known him very long.

I have a private room, which is nice because it means I can have visitors in here without anyone else around. I have a television and my own phone too. I don't watch TV all that much unless I'm really bored but I use the phone a lot. Randy calls me in the morning and comes over every afternoon and then calls again every evening. We usually talk until bedtime, or later, but the nurses don't say anything. Some of them have told me that my boyfriend is cute, although I'm not sure if they really think that or they're just saying it to be nice.

I've had quite a few visitors already, and everyone has been really nice.

Mrs. Wickholm came and brought me some magazines and a huge fruit basket that had some fruits in it that I've never even seen before. I thought that was really cool because this is my last chance to try new things like that.

Maryanne came too and I was really proud of her. It was the first time that she's been anywhere that actually counts as a public place. I don't count my house because it was just the family, but this is different. She mentioned that Mrs. Wickholm has hired her to redecorate — and not just a few rooms but her whole house.

Josie came over twice and brought me a beautiful copy of *Pride and Prejudice* by Jane Austen. I love Jane Austen's books because of the way characters talk all formal and everything. It would have been cool to live back then, and talk that way, though I think wearing those dumb long dresses must have been a real drag.

I told Josie that I want her to have my teddy bear collection and she cried and cried and told me not to talk that way. Josie isn't very practical sometimes. I pointed out that I'm not going to be needing them and it would mean a lot to me if she had them, but that just made her cry more. Anyway, I let Momma know so she can give them to Josie after it's all over.

Momma has been amazing. I know how hard this must be for her, but she's so strong and brave and that helps me to be strong too. Daddy tries hard, but it seems he has more trouble handling all of this than Momma. I guess that's because he always protected me from things and now he can't.

I remember when I was small I used to get up on his shoulders and he'd carry me around and I felt like I could see the whole world from up there. I thought I was safe when I was with my Daddy, no matter what happened. I thought if a robber ever broke into our house, Daddy would capture him easily, or if a big old bear ever came along when we were camping at the lake, Daddy would just kill it with his bare hands.

We used to go fishing together, at first just Daddy and me, and then later on Mark would come too. It took me years to figure out why I always caught more fish than he did. He said I was a better fisherman, but eventually I realized that every time he had a nibble on his line he'd tell me he needed a rest and would get me to trade poles, because his was bigger. The next thing I'd be reeling in a fish and gloating at how fast I'd caught one when he'd been waiting all that time for nothing.

Of course when I accused him of this, he denied it. But his eyes were twinkling, which is always a dead give-away with Daddy. He's not very good at hiding things.

I did fun things with Momma too, but mostly more practical things. She taught me how to cook a lot of different foods — although the kitchen would look like a disaster area when I was done. I remember once when I was making pancakes I flipped one and it flew out of the pan and right onto the floor. Momma scraped it up and told me she thought it was a little undercooked on one side and we laughed and laughed.

I'd insist on doing everything by myself and she never tried to take over. I'd crack eggs that slimed down the counter or spill flour all over the place and she'd just stand by and help me fix my mistakes. But she never criticized or complained.

It's been such a huge blessing to have my parents. If a person has to die at fourteen, well, I guess it's easier if their life has been filled with love and happiness. I know a lot of my friends seem to be waiting for their lives to start. They talk about what they're going to do when they're older as though that's when life will actually begin. It's like they're waiting for the time when they can be happy. I've had that all my life.

I've had a good life.

~

I try to write a little each day, but yesterday I was too sick to lift my head off the pillow. I don't really like it when they give me needles for pain and stuff, because it makes me woozy and light-headed and I can't concentrate on anything.

When Randy was here yesterday he was so kind and understanding. I couldn't talk much and he just sat for hours and held my hand.

The nurses don't say anything when I have more company than you're supposed to. I think patients are only allowed two visitors at a time, but yesterday there was Randy and Momma and Daddy and Mark and Josie all at the same time and the nurse just said to make sure I wasn't overtired.

Daddy and Randy had a big talk the other day. Not here, though, Randy went to the house to see Daddy, and Momma told me that they had a great conversation and Daddy thinks he's a fine young man now. I'm glad about that. I knew Daddy would like Randy if he got a chance to get to know him.

~

My doctor looked really grim today.

~

Things aren't so clear anymore. I find it hard to write anything because my head is all fuzzy and my thoughts keep getting all jumbled and confused. I start to think about something and the next thing there's a whole different thought going through my mind. It's like there's a chaotic party of my life playing itself in my head.

~

Momma brought me bouquets of fresh-cut flowers from our garden today. I don't think there can be any left there because after we filled the vases she'd brought along, there were still quite a lot left. We had to use some plastic cups from the cafeteria for some of the smaller flowers.

They're so pretty, all lined up, sitting on the windowsill. It's like a huge burst of living colours, waving and nodding. I feel as though my room is full of dancing smiles.

I wish they could last forever.